Mississippi River Tales

McSherry
Waugh
Greenberg

Mississippi River Tales

From the American Storytelling Tradition

Edited by Frank McSherry, Jr., Charles G. Waugh
& Martin Harry Greenberg

August House / *Little Rock*
PUBLISHERS

Printed in the United States of America

10 9 8 7 6 5 4 3 2 1

LIBRARY OF CONGRESS CATALOGING-IN-PUBLICATION DATA

Mississippi river tales
edited by Frank D. McSherry, Jr., Charles G.
Waugh, and Martin H. Greenberg. — 1st ed.
p.   cm.
ISBN 0-87483-067-2 (pbk.)   : $8.95
1. Mississippi River — Fiction.
2. Mississippi River Valley — Fiction.
3. Short stories, American.
I. McSherry, Frank D. II. Waugh, Charles.
III. Greenberg, Martin Harry.
PS648.M46M57   1988
813'.01'083277 — dc 19   88-17554
                                                                CIP

First Edition, 1988

Cover illustration by Jan Weeks
Production artwork by Ira Hocut
Typography by Diversified Graphics, Little Rock, Arkansas
Design direction by Ted Parkhurst
Project direction by Hope Norman Coulter

This book is printed on archival-quality paper which meets the
guidelines for performance and durability of the Committee
on Production Guidelines for Book Longevity of the Council
on Library Resources.

AUGUST HOUSE, INC.   PUBLISHERS   LITTLE ROCK

Contents

Acknowledgments

"Jesus Knew" by E.P. O'Donnell, copyright 1935 by *Harper's Magazine*. All rights reserved. Reprinted from the April issue by special permission.

"Maud Island" by Erskine Caldwell, reprinted by permission of Dodd, Mead & Company, Inc., from *Stories of Life North and South* by Erskine Caldwell. Copyright 1934 by Erskine Caldwell. Copyright © renewed 1962 by Erskine Caldwell.

"On the Lake" by Ellen Douglas, copyright © 1961 by Ellen Douglas. First appeared in *The New Yorker*, August 26, 1961. Reprinted by permission of Christine K. Tomasino, Robert Lewis Rosen Associates, Ltd.

"Philo Gubb's Greatest Case" by Ellis Parker Butler, from *Philo Gubb* by Ellis Parker Butler. Copyright 1913, 1914, and 1915 by The Red Book Corporation. Copyright 1918 by Ellis Parker Butler. Copyright © renewed by Ida Anna Butler. Reprinted by permission of Houghton Mifflin Company.

"Ram Him, Damn Him!" by H. Bedford-Jones, copyright by the Estate of H. Bedford-Jones. Reprinted by permission of the agents for the author's Estate, the Scott Meredith Literary Agency, Inc., 845 Third Avenue, New York, NY 10022.

"Stillwater, 1896" by Michael Cassutt, copyright © 1984 by Michael Cassutt. By permission of the author. First published in *Shadows 7*.

Introduction

Half twain! Quarter twain! M-a-r-k twain!

from **Mark Twain,**

Life on the Mississippi

What fascinating scenes that phrase re-creates! A river-man kneeling in the prow of a steamer on a warm, starshot night, swinging a lead weight on a line to deter-mine the majestic river's depth ahead. Sleepy towns lining the long brown length of the stream, sparkling in the sunlight, as the great riverboats loom into view, floating palaces painted gold and scarlet, two and three stories high, tall-stacked . . . with names that echo yet — the *Natchez,* the *Tuscarora,* the *Robert E. Lee* — the *General Quitman* and the *Belle of the West.* Floating ahead of them comes the music — for the riverboat steamers carried not only cotton and lumber but culture — *"Here comes the showboat!"* — with its bouncy, banjo-jangling, tambourine-tapping, riverboat rhythm.

The magic spell of that mighty river is a vivid setting for colorful stories, used by such authors as Edna Ferber, creator of the famous novel and musical *Showboat* with its immortal Hammerstein and Kerns score that includes "Old Man River"; and Mark Twain — himself a riverboat pilot in those glory days before the Civil War when a Mis-sissippi River pilot was "the only unfettered and entirely independent human being that lived on the earth . . . I loved that profession," said Twain, "far better than any I have followed since."

Yet there's something else that appeals in *Mississippi River Tales,* something particularly American. For that

7

river helped to make us what we are today.

For one thing, it helped make Americans rich and powerful by the standards of the rest of the world. The first European to see the river was the Spanish explorer Hernando de Soto in 1542, who was buried in its bosom. It was more than a century later before Robert Cavalier de la Salle explored the Mississippi from its northern heights near Itasca, where it drops 1,670 feet to begin its journey of more than a thousand miles — 3,986 to be exact — to its southern end past New Orleans and into the Gulf of Mexico. The first steamer did not appear on it until 1811 — but by the decade before the Civil War the Americans had more than 3,000 steamers on the Mississippi. Machinery and lumber going south, cotton and rice going north, and wealth going with it all.

(Slaves, too, were sold. On a trip that changed American history, Abraham Lincoln took a flatboat down the river to New Orleans, saw the horror of slavery firsthand and decided to destroy it if he ever got the chance; a few years later he did.)

Searoads of commerce are highways of war; the importance of the Mississippi was shown once again during the Civil War. In 1863 Union General U.S. Grant took the Confederate river fortress of Vicksburg, and with it control of the Missisippi. The act cut the Confederacy in two. Supplies for the enemy, from the great plains west of the mighty river — horses and forage for the cavalry, bacon and beef for the infantry — stopped, the Confederate armies began to starve, and the end was in sight. "The Father of Waters," said President Abraham Lincoln, "now flows unvexed to the sea."

The Mississippi helped build our national character, for it is a rowdy river, rambunctious and unpredictable, like us. In full flood tide that river can sweep away a 40-acre farm a minute and can cut off 30-mile-wide chunks of land; in the giant 1926 flood it left a quarter-million people homeless, and New Orleans saved itself only by dynamiting its levees to let the roaring waters rocket into the Gulf.

into the Gulf.

Catastrophes like those teach us how to cope and rebuild. Such disasters demonstrate, says English traveller James Morris in *As I Saw the U.S.A.,* "the surprising American resilience to disaster." He observes that "fierce strokes of fortune are in the blood of Americans, and they accept them . . . without much fuss."

The Mississippi helped to teach us that.

The river is, in short, much like Americans — strong, big, possessed of the means of weath, and generous with them. But the river is also unpredictable and violent. And that's us, too, unfortunately: "a strain of violence," Morris notes, "emboldens the American character." He believes that some of it is due to our "tigerish environment."

Perhaps it is this that accounts for the appeal fo the majestic Mississippi in fiction. It symbolizes us.

We hope you enjoy the stories included here. We've picked them for color and variety; there's "Ram Him, Damn Him!", a fast-moving tale of Civil War battle action between river steamers by the popular and prolific pulp author, H. Bedford-Jones, famous for his historical adventures; comedy in the story of detective "Philo Gubb's Greatest Case," by humorist Ellis Parker Butler; grim horror in Irvin Cobb's "Fishhead," set in an eerie landscape formed by a Mississippi rampage; and dramas of love and revenge, struggles for survival, and simply growing-up.

There are not only regional stories. They are stories about us, about the American character.

Turn the page then — for —

Here comes the showboat!

Frank D. McSherry Jr.

Stillwater, 1896

MICHAEL CASSUTT

They are big families up here on the St. Croix. I myself am the second of eight, and ours was the smallest family of any on Chestnut Street. You might think we were all hard-breeding Papists passing as Lutherans, but I have since learned that it is due to the long winters. For fifty years I have been hearing that Science will take care of winters just like we took care of the river, with our steel high bridge and diesel-powered barges that go the size of a football field. But every damn November the snow falls again and in spring the river swells from bluff to bluff. The loggers can be heard cursing all the way from Superior. I alone know that this is because of what we done to John Jeremy.

I was just a boy then, short of twelve, that would be in 1896, and by mutual agreement of little use to anyone, not my father nor my brothers nor my departed mother. I knew my letters, to be sure, and could be trusted to appear at Church in a clean collar, but my primary achievement at that age was to be known as the best junior logroller in the county, a title I had won the previous Fourth of July, beating boys from as far away as Rice Lake and Taylors Falls. In truth, I tended to lollygag when sent to Kinnick's Store, never failing to take a detour down to the riverfront, where a Mississippi excursion boat like the *Verne Swain* or the *Kalitan,* up from St. Louis or New Orleans, would be pulled in. I had the habit of getting into snowball fights on my way to school, and was notorious for one whole winter as the boy who almost put out Oscar Tolz's eye with a missile into which I had embedded a small pebble. (Oscar Tolz was a God damned Swede and a bully to boot.) Often I would not get to school at all. This did not vex my father to any great degree, as he had only a year of schooling himself. It mightily vexed my elder brother, Dolph. I can still recall him appearing like an avenging angel wherever I went, it seemed, saying, "Peter, what in God's name are you doing there? Get away from there!" Dolph was all of fourteen at the time and ambitious, having been promised a job at the Hersey Bean Lumberyard when the Panic ended. He was also suspicious of my frivolous associates, particularly one named John Jeremy.

I now know that John Jeremy was the sort of man you meet on the river — bearded, unkempt, prone to sudden, mystifying exclamations and gestures. The better folk got no further with him, while curious boys found him somewhat more interesting, perhaps because of his profession. "I'm descended from the line of St. Peter himself," he told me once. "Do you know why?"

I drew the question because my given name is Peter. "Because you are a fisher of men," I told him.

Truth, in the form of hard liquor, was upon John Jeremy that day. He amended my phrase: "A fisher of dead men." John Jeremy fished for corpses.

He had been brought up from Chicago, they said, in 1885 by the Hersey family itself. Whether motivated by a series of personal losses or by some philanthropic spasm I do not know, having been otherwise occupied at the time. I found few who were able or willing to discuss the subject when at last I sprouted interest. I do know that a year did not pass then that the St. Croix did not take at least half a dozen people to its shallow bottom. This in a town of less than six hundred, though that figure was subject to constant change due to riverboats and loggers who, I think, made up a disproportionate amount of the tribute. You can not imagine the distress a drowning caused in those days. Now part of this was normal human grief (most of the victims were children), but much of it, I have come to believe, was a deep revulsion in the knowledge that the source of our drinking water, the heart of our livelihood — the river! — was fouled by the bloating, gassy corpse of someone we all knew. There was nothing rational about it, but the fear was real nonetheless: when the whistle at the courthouse blew, you ran for it, for either the town was on fire, or somebody was breathing river.

Out would go the rowboats, no matter what the weather or time of night, filled with farmers unused to water with their weights, poles, nets, and hopes. It was tedious, sad, and unrewarding work . . . except for a specialist like John Jeremy.

"You stay the hell away from that man," Dolph hissed at me one day. "I've seen you hanging around down there with him. He's the Devil himself."

Normally, a statement like this from Dolph would have served only to encourage further illicit association, but none was actually needed. I had come across John Jeremy for the first time that spring, idly fishing at a spot south of town near the lumberyard. It was not the best fishing hole, if you used worms or other unimaginative bait, for the St. Croix was low that year, as it had been for ten years, and the fish were fat with bugs easily caught in the shallows. I had picked up a marvelous invention known as the casting fly and had applied it that spring with great success. And I was only too happy to share the

13

secret with a thin, pale, scruffy fellow who looked as if he had skipped meals of late. We introduced ourselves and proceeded to take a goodly number of crappies and sunfish during the afternoon. "That's quite a trick you got there," John Jeremy told me. "You make that up all by yourself?"

I confessed that I had read about it in a dime novel, though if Oscar Tolz had asked me, I would have lied. John Jeremy laughed, showing that his teeth were a match for the rest of his ragged appearance.

"Well, it works good enough. Almost makes me wish I'd learned how to read."

By this point, as I remember it, we had hiked up to the Afton Road and were headed back to Stillwater. As we walked, I was struck by John Jeremy's thinness and apparent ill health, and in a fit of Christian charity — I was just twelve — I offered him some of my catch, which was far larger than his.

John Jeremy regarded me for a moment. I think he was amused. "Aren't you a rascal, Peter Gollwitzer. Thank you, but no. In spite of the fact that it's been a long dry spell, I'm still able to feed myself, though it don't show. I'll grant you that. In fact, in exchange for your kindness" — his voice took on a conspiratorial tone — "I shall reward you with this." And into my hand he pressed a five-dollar gold piece. "For the secret of the fly, eh? Now run along home."

My father was unamused by my sudden wealth, especially when he learned the source. "That man is worse than a grave robber. He profits through the misfortune of others." It was then that I learned John Jeremy's true profession, and that he had been known to charge as much as *five hundred dollars* for a single "recovery," as it was called. "One time, I swear by the Lord," my father continued, "he *refused* to turn over a body he had recovered because the payment wasn't immediately forthcoming! A man like that is unfit for human company." I reserved judgment, clutching the eagle in my sweaty palm, happier than I would have been with a chestful of pirate treasure.

June is a month to be remembered for tornados, with the wind screaming and trees falling and the river churning. In this instance there was a riverboat, the *Sidney,* taking a side trip from St. Paul — and regretting it — putting into town just as one of those big blowers hit. One of her deckhands, a Negro, was knocked into the water. Of course, none of those people can swim, and in truth I doubt Jonah himself could have got out of those waters that day. The courthouse whistle blew, though it was hard to hear over the roar of the wind, and Dolph (who had been sent home from the yard) grabbed my arm and tugged me toward the docks.

The crowd there was bigger than you'd expect, given the weather — not only townspeople, but many from the *Sidney,* who were quite vocal in their concern about the unfortunate blackamoor. Into our midst came John Jeremy, black gunnysack — he referred to it as his "bag of tricks" — over his shoulder. People stepped aside, the way they do for the sheriff, letting him pass. He sought out the *Sidney*'s captain. I took it that they were haggling over the price, since the captain's voice presently rose above the storm: "I've never heard such an outrage in my life!" But an agreement was reached and soon, in the middle of the storm, we saw John Jeremy put out in his skiff. It was almost dark by then and the corpse fisher, floating with the wind-whipped water with all the seeming determination of a falling leaf, disappeared from our sight.

The onlookers began to drift home then while the passengers from the *Sidney* headed up the street in search of a warm, dry tavern. Dolph and I and the younger ones — including Oscar Tolz — stayed behind. Because of my familiarity with the corpse fisher I was thought to have intimate and detailed knowledge of his

15

techniques, which, they say, he refused to discuss. "I bet he uses loafs of bread," one boy said. "Like in Mark Twain."

"Don't be a dope," Oscar Tolz said. "Books are not real. My old man says he's got animals in that sack. Some kind of trained rats — maybe muskrats."

"Like hell," said a third. "I saw that sack and there was nothing alive in it. Muskrats would be squirming to beat the band."

"Maybe they're *drowned* muskrats," I offered, earning a cuff from Dolph. Normally, that would have been my signal to shut my mouth, as Dolph's sense of humor — never notable — was not presently on duty. But that evening, for some reason, I felt immune. I asked him, "Okay, Dolph, what do *you* think he uses?"

One thing Dolph always liked was a technical question. He immediately forgot that he was annoyed with me. "I think," he said after a moment, "that John Jeremy's got some sort of compass." Before anyone could laugh, he raised his hand. "Now just you remember this: all the strange machines people got nowadays. If they got a machine that can make pictures move and another one can say words, how hard can it be to make a compass that instead of finding north finds dead people?"

This sounded so eminently reasonable to all of us that we promptly clasped the idea to us with a fervor of which our parents — having seen us bored in Church — thought us incapable. The boy who knew Mark Twain's stories suggested that this compass must have been invented by Thomas Edison, and who was to dispute that? Oscar Tolz announced that John Jeremy — who was known to have traveled a bit — might have busted Tom Edison in the noggin and stolen the compass away, which was why he had it and no one else did. "Especially since Edison's been suffering from amnesia ever since," I said. I confess that we grew so riotous that we did not notice how late it had gotten and that John Jeremy's laden skiff was putting in to the dock. We took one good look at the hulking and life-less cargo coming toward us and scurried away like mice.

Later I felt ashamed, because of what John Jeremy must have wondered, and because there was no real reason for us to run. A body drowned, at most, three hours could not have transformed into one of those horrors we had all heard about. It was merely the body of a poor dead black man.

I learned that John Jeremy had earned one hundred dollars for his work that afternoon, plus a free dinner with the captain of the *Sidney*. Feelings in Stillwater ran quite hot against this for some days, since one hundred dollars was the amount Reverend Bickell earned in a year for saving souls.

Over the Fourth I successfully defended my junior logrolling title; that, combined with other distractions, prevented me from seeing John Jeremy until one afternoon in early August. He was balancing unsteadily on the end of the dock, obviously drunk, occasionally cupping his hand to his ear as if listening to some faroff voice, flapping his arms to right himself.

He did not strike me as a mean or dangerous drunk (such a drinker was my father, rest his soul), just unhappy. "Florida!" he announced abruptly. "Florida, Alabama, Mississippi, Missouri, Illinois, Michigan, Wisconsin, here." He counted the state on his hand. "And never welcome anywhere for long, Peter. Except Stillwater. Why do you suppose that is?'

"Maybe it is better here."

John Jeremy laughed loudly. "I wouldn't have thought to say that, but maybe it is, by God." He coughed. "Maybe it's because I've kept the river quiet . . . and folks appreciate it." He saw none-too-fleeting disdain on my face. "True! By God, when was the last time the St. Croix went over its banks? Tell me when! Eighteen eighty-four is when! One year before the disreputable John Jeremy showed his ugly face in the quiet town of Stillwater. Not one flood in that time, sir! I stand on my record." He almost fell on it, as he was seized with another wheezing cough.

"Then the city should honor you," I said helpfully. "You should be the mayor."

"Huh! You're too innocent, Peter. A corpse fisher for mayor. No sir, the Christian folk will not have *that*. Better a brewer, or a usurer — or the undertaker!"

He had gotten quite loud, and much as I secretly enjoyed my friendship with him, I recognized truth in what he said.

"You wouldn't want to be mayor, anyway."

He shook his head, grinning. "No. After all, what mayor can do what *I* do, eh? Who speaks to the river like I do? No one." He paused and was quiet, then added, "No one else is strong enough to pay the price."

Though I was far from tired of this conversation, I knew, from extensive experience with my father, that John Jeremy would likely grow steadily less coherent. I tried to help him to his feet, quite an achievement given my stature at the time, and, as he lapsed into what seemed to be a sullen silence, guided him toward his shack.

I was rewarded with a look inside. In the dark, I confess, I expected a magic compass, or muskrat cages, but all that I beheld were the possessions of a drifter: a gunnysack, a pole, some weights, and a net. I left John Jeremy among them, passed out on his well-worn cot.

Four days later, on a Saturday afternoon, in the thick, muggy heat of August, the courthouse whistle blew. I was on my way home from Kinnick's, having run an errand for my father, and made a quick detour downtown. Oscar Tolz was already there, shouting, "Someone's drowned at the lumberyard!" I was halfway there before I remembered that Dolph was working.

The sawmill at the Hersey Bean Lumberyard sat on pilings well into the St. Croix, the better to deal with the river of wood that floated its way every spring and summer. It was a God damned treacherous place, especially when huge timbers were being pulled in and swung to face the blades. Dolph had been knocked off because he had not ducked in time.

The water was churning that day beneath the mill in spite of the lack of wind and current. I suspect it had to do with the peculiar set of the pilings and the movements of the big logs. At any rate, Dolph, a strong swimmer, had been hurled into an obstruction, possibly striking his head, so observers said. He had gone under the water then, not to be seen again.

The shoreline just to the south of the yard was rugged and overgrown. It was possible that Dolph, knocked senseless for a moment, had been carried that way where, revived, he could swim to safety, unbeknownst to the rest of us. Some men went to search there.

It was told there was nothing I could do, and to tell the truth, I was glad. My father arrived and without saying a word to me went off with the searchers. He had lost a wife and child already.

John Jeremy arrived. He had his gunnysack over his shoulder and an oar in his hand. Behind him two men hauled his skiff. I stood up to meet him, I'm ashamed to say, wiping tears on my pantaloons. I had the presence of mind to know that there was business to be conducted.

"This is all I have," I told him, holding out the five-dollar gold piece I had carried for weeks.

I saw real pain in his eyes. The breath itself seemed to seep out of him. "This will be on the house," he said finally. He patted me on the shoulder with a hand that was glazed and hard, and went down to the river.

My father's friends took me away then and put some food in me, and made me look after the other children. I fell asleep early that warm evening and, not surprisingly, woke while it was still dark, frightened and confused. Had they found him? I wanted to know, and with my father still not home, I had no one to ask.

Dressing, I sneaked out and walked down to the lumberyard. The air was hot and heavy even though dawn was not far off . . . so hot that even the bugs were quiet. I made my way to the dock and sat there, listening to the lazy slap of the water.

There was a slice of moon in the sky, and by its light it seemed that I could see a skiff slowly crossing back and forth, back and forth, between two prominent coves to the south. A breeze came up all of a sudden, a breeze that chilled but did not cool, hissing in the reeds like a faraway voice. I fell forward on my hands and shouted into the darkness: "Who's there?"

No one answered. Perhaps it was all a dream. I do know that eventually the sky reddened on the Wisconsin side and I was able to clearly see John Jeremy's distant skiff.

Hungry now and deadly sure of my own uselessness in the affair, I drifted home and got something to eat. It was very quiet in the house. My father was home, but tired, and he offered nothing. I went out to Church voluntarily, and prayed for once, alone.

Almost hourly during that Sunday I went down to the St. Croix. Each time, I was able to spot John Jeremy, infinitely patient in his search.

It finally occurred to me about mid-afternoon that I had to do something to help, even if it came to naught. Leaving the house again, I walked past the lumberyard toward the brushy shallows where John Jeremy was, hoping that in some way my sorry presence would encourage a merciful God to end this. I was frankly terrified of what I would see — a body drowned a goodly time and in August heat at that — yet anxious to confront it, to move *past* it and get on with other business.

Two hours of beating through the underbrush, occasionally stepping into the green scum at water's edge, exhausted me. I believe I sat down for a while and cried, and presently I felt better — better enough to continue.

It was almost sunset. The sun had crossed to the Minnesota side and dipped toward the trees on the higher western bluffs, casting eerie shadows in the coves. Perhaps that is why I did not see them until I was almost upon them.

There, in the shallow water, among the cattails and scum, was John Jeremy's skiff. In it was a huge white thing that once was my brother Dolph. The sight was every bit as horrific as I had imagined, and even across an expanse of water the smell rivaled the pits of Hell . . . but that alone, I can honestly say, did not make me scream. It was another thing that made me call out, an image I will carry to my grave, of John Jeremy pressing his ear to the greenish lips of my brother's corpse.

My scream started him. "Peter!" he yelled. I was as incapable of locomotion as the cattails that separated us. John Jeremy raised himself and began to pole toward me. "Peter, wait for me."

I found my voice, weak though it was. "What are you doing to my brother?"

He beached his nightmare cargo and stumbled out of the skiff. He was frantic, pleading, out of breath. "Don't run, Peter, hear me out."

I managed to back up, putting some distance between us. "Stay away!"

"I told you, Peter, I talk to the river. I *listen* to it, too." He nodded towards Dolph's body. "They tell me where the next one will be found, Peter, so I can get them out, because the river doesn't want them for long — "

I clapped my hands over my ears and screamed again, backing away as fast as I could. The slope was against me, though, and I fell.

John Jeremy held out his hand. "I could teach you the secret, Peter. You have the gift. You could learn it easy."

For a long second, perhaps a heartbeat and a half, I stared at his grimy hand. But a gentle wave lapped at the skiff and the God-awful creaking broke his spell. I turned and scurried up the hill. Reaching the top, I remembered the gold piece in my pocket. I took it out and threw it at him.

At twelve your secrets do not keep. Eventually, some ver-

sion of what I'd seen and told got around town, and it
went hard with John Jeremy. Stillwater's version of tar-
and-feathering was to gang up on a man, kick the hell out
of him, and drag him as far south as he could be dragged,
possessions be damned. I was not there. Sometimes, as I
think back, I fool myself into believing that I was . . . that
John Jeremy forgave me, like Christ forgave his tor-
mentors. But that did not happen.

Eventually, we learned that John Jeremy's "secret"
was actually a special three-pronged hook attached to a
weight that could be trolled on a river bottom. Any fool
could find a body, they said. Maybe so.

But the flood of '97 damned near killed Stillwater and
things haven't improved since then. A day don't go by
now that I don't think of John Jeremy's secret and wish
I'd said yes. Especially when I go down to the river and
hear the water rustling in the reeds, making that awful
sound, the sound I keep telling myself is not the voices of
the dead.

Weenokhenchah Wandeeteekah

WILLIAM JOSEPH SNELLING

She bore her wrongs in deep and silent sorrow;
Endured the anguish of a broken heart
In uncomplaining sadness; saw her love
Repaid with cold neglect. But stung at last
To the bosom's inmost core, she tried the sole
Effectual remedy despair had left her.

UNPUBLISHED PLAY.

Shortly after the *coureurs des bois* began to carry packs
and drive dog sledges in the lands on the upper waters of
the Mississippi, there lived at the Kahpozhah village,
three leagues below the mouth of the river St Peters, an
Indian who was the cynosure of the eyes of all the
maidens in his band. This was because of his rare personal beauty; not of form, for that is common to all
Indians; but of countenance. His skill as a hunter, and
his bravery as a warrior, were qualities more likely to
recommend him to their parents; but strange to say, the

swarthy daughters of the forest judged by the eye, as some authors have falsely asserted their sex is in the habit of doing. The object of their admiration had feminine features, and a skin lighter by five shades than the national complexion of the Dahcotahs, and his hair, beside being light, was also fine and glossy. He prided himself upon it, and suffered it to grow long; thereby grievously scandalizing the male population of the village. His toilet was usually adjusted with scrupulous accuracy; he changed the fashion of his paint five times per diem, and his activity in the chase enabled him to wear so much scarlet cloth, and so many beads and silver broaches, as made him the envy of those of his own age and sex. Those who imagine that the aborigines are all stoics and heroes, and those who think them solely addicted to rapine and bloodshed, and are therefore disposed to dispute the truth of this sketch of Indian character, are informed that there are fops in the forest as well as in Broadway, their intrinsic value pretty much the same in both places. The beau of the Northwest arranges his locks, and stains his face with mud, by a looking-glass three inches square. He of the city submits his equally empty head to the hand of a friseur, and powders his visage before a mirror in a gilt frame, in which he can behold his estimable person at full length. The former arrays his person with scarlet, and covers his feet with deer skin and porcupine quills; and the other gets a coat from Cox, whose needle, it is said, has pierced more hearts than the shaft of Cupid; and his feet prove the merits of Day and Martin. The only difference we see between the two is, that the savage kills deer and buffaloes, and helps to support his family, while the white man is often a useless member of society. Yet the elegance of the features of Toskatnay (the Woodpecker), for so was our Dahcotah dandy called, and his taste in dress, were not his only merits. The war eagle's plume which completed his array, was an honorable evidence that he had acquired a right to call himself a man. In fact, beneath an almost feminine appearance, and much frivolity of manner, he concealed the real strength of his character. To the maidens who listened with glistening eyes to his discourse, and blushed when he addressed them, his motto seemed to be, "let them look and die." Exquisite as he was, his soul was full of higher matters than love or gallantry. He aspired to sway the councils of his people, and to lead them in battle, and if he condescended to please the eyes, and tickle the ears of the women, it was only because he knew that it was the surest way to exert an influence over the men. He was not so much of a savage as not to know so much of human nature. Yet he had no idea of marrying, but as it might further his views; and to the admiration of the young squaws he shut his eyes, while against their complaints that "no one cared for them," he hardened his heart.

With all his schemes, he had not calculated upon the power of the blind god, as indeed, how should he, having never heard of such a personage? The passion of which that deity is a type, he scarcely believed to exist, certainly never expected to feel. But his time was to come, and the connexion he was destined to form, was to have a powerful influence on his future fortunes. We are thus particular in detailing his conduct and feelings, in order that our own countrymen may take warning, and profit by his example. There is a use to be found for everything, however mean, and he who flirts with the brunettes and blondes that congregate at Ballston or Saratoga, need not shame to take a lesson from a Dahcotah warrior.

In the same village with our hero dwelt a damsel, whose name, as it has not come down to us, being lost in the exploit of which this true history treats, we cannot tell, and shall therefore speak of her as Weenokhenchah Wandeeteekah (the Brave Woman), the appellation which her tribe give her, in relating the story. This girl never praised Toskatnay's attire, nor listened to his compliments, nor sought to attract his attention. On the contrary, she avoided his notice. Why she did thus, we do not pretend to explain. We pretend not to expound the freaks of passion, any more than the profundities of philosophy, nor can we tell why love should choose to show himself in such a capricious manner. Let it suffice that she was thought to hate our hero until an event occurred that contradicted the supposition.

One hot day in July, a rabid wolf, such as are sometimes seen in the prairies, came to pay the village a visit. The cornfields lay in his way, and as animals in his predicament never turn aside, he entered it. It so chanced that Weenokhenchah Wandeeteekah was at that time using her hoe therein, in company with other girls, while Toskatnay stood near them, cheering their labor and edifying their minds, pretty much in the style of Ranger in the Jealous Husband. The wolf made directly at him, and the girls seeing by the slaver of his jaws, what ailed him, shrieked and fled. Toskatnay, being no Yankee, could not guess the cause of their terror, and was looking about for it, when the animal was within five paces of him. Weenokhenchah Wandeeteekah alone stood firm, and seeing that he must inevitably be bitten, she advanced and clove the beast's skull with her hoe, contrary to the law in such cases made and provided by novel writers, which ordains that the gentleman shall rescue the lady from danger, and not the lady the gentleman. Having thus done, the color forsook her cheeks, and she swooned and fell.

Toskatnay, though an Indian fine gentleman, did not catch her in his arms, nor kneel by her. But he did what was as much to the purpose. He ran to the village, which was but a few rods distant, and sent the women to her assistance. With some difficulty they brought her to her senses.

From that hour his attentions, which had before been considered by the girls as common property, were confined to her. Love and gratitude prevailed, and for a while his dreams of ambition were forgotten. He wore leggings of different colors, and sat all day upon a log, playing on a flute with three holes, and singing songs in her praise. When she was gone to cut wood, he was not to be found in the village. He gave her beads and vermilion, and in short played the Indian lover in all points. Indian courtships never last long, and ere the leaves began to fall, Weenokhenchah Wandeeteekah was the wedded wife of Toskatnay. For a time, he forgot his nature and his former prepossessions, and he even saw three war parties leave the village without testifying much concern. But these halcyon days did not last long. A mind like his could not be content with ignoble triumphs over the brute tenants of the woods and prairies. His excursions grew longer in duration, and more frequent in occurrence, and at last the poor bride saw herself totally neglected. Another cause concurred in this result. She belonged to a family that could boast no hero, no chief, nor any wise man among its members, and her husband saw with regret that he had formed an alliance that could never enhance his importance in his tribe. The devoted affection, and unwearied attention with which she endeavored to recall his heart, only filled him with disgust. Within the year she made him a father, but the new relation in which he stood, did not reclaim him. In the eyes of his people, he pursued a more honorable course: he joined every warlike excursion, obtained the praise of all by his valor; and once by his conduct and presence of mind, when the camp in which his lodge was pitched was surprised, he saved it, and turned the tables on the assailants. In consequence, he was thought worthy to be a leader of men, and became the head partizan in two successful inroads on the enemies' country.

He was envied as well as admired. Many there were, older than himself, who aspired to the objects of his ambition, and one in especial, without a tithe of his merits, outstripped him in his course by means of extended connections, and thwarted him in every particular. This was a man named Chahpah (the Beaver), about forty years of age. He had nine wives, whom he supported in the usual

27

style, and their relations were at his beck. Jealous of the
growing influence of Toskatnay, he opposed his opinions,
and turned the weak parts of his character into ridicule.
The young warrior felt this deeply, and revolved in his
own mind the means of making the number of his
adherents equal to that of his rival. There were two ways
presented themselves to his acceptance; the one to take
to his lodge more wives; and the other, to continue to
exert himself in the field. By the latter means, in the
course of time, if he was not untimely cut off, he would
attain the desired distinction. By the former his object
would be effected more speedily.

An opportunity soon occurred to measure his strength
with his fellow aspirant. The Beaver, not content with
the limits of his harem, demanded in marriage the
daughter of the Heron, a noted warrior. The father asked
time to consider the proposal. While the matter was in
abeyance, Toskatnay heard of it, and resolved not to lose
so good a chance to further his own projects and mortify
the man he hated. He went that very night to the Heron's
lodge, lighted a match at his fire, and presented it to the
eyes of the maiden. She blew it out, and after some conversation with her, carried on in whispers, he retired. In
the morning he smoked with the Heron, and in plain
terms asked his daughter to wife. The old man liked
Toskatnay, and moreover, was not entirely satisfied that
his offspring should be the tenth bride of any man. He ac-
cepted the offer without hesitation, and the nuptials
were solemnized forthwith, to the great displeasure of
the Beaver.

It is unnecessary to say that he was not the only person
displeased. Weenokhenchah Wandeeteekah thought this
second marriage a poor requital of the service she had
rendered her husband, and expostulated with him. But
ambition swallows all other passions, as the rod of Moses
swallowed the other rods, and Toskatnay had become
intensely selfish. He desired her to mind her own affairs,
and as polygamy is reckoned creditable by the Dahco-

tahs, she had no pretence to quarrel, and was obliged to submit. With an aching heart, she saw another woman take the place in Toskatnay's regard that she considered her own, and often did she retire to the woods to weep over her infant, and tell her sorrows to the rocks and trees. Quarrels will happen in the best of families, and so was seen of Toskatnay's. The two wives did not agree, as might have been expected, and the husband always took the part of the new comer. Moreover, when he joined the hunting camps, the Heron's daughter accompanied him, while Weenokhenchah Wandeeteekah was left at home; he alleging, that having a child to take care of, she could not so well be the partner of his wanderings. It was in vain that she protested against this reasoning. An Indian husband is, if he pleases, absolute, and she was obliged to acquiesce. It was not, in truth, that he preferred his new spouse, but he wished to conciliate her family. The poor malcontent had the mortification besides, to see that he neglected his child, and this was the unkindest cut of all.

At last, the second autumn after her marriage, it so happened that the band attached to Toskatnay was to move up the Mississippi, and hunt upon its head waters. As the journey was to be made by water, there was no objection to Weenokhenchah Wandeeteekah being of the party, and the two wives assisted each other in the neces-sary preparations. In the afternoon they came to the falls of St Anthony, and carried their canoes and baggage round it. They encamped on the eastern shore just above the rapids. Such a description as we are able to give of this celebrated cataract, from recollection, is at the reader's service.

There is nothing of the grandeur or sublimity which the eye aches to behold at Niagara, about the falls of St Anthony. But in wild and picturesque beauty it is per-haps unequalled. Flowing over a tract of country five hundred miles in extent, the river, here more than half a mile wide, breaks into sheets of foam and rushes to the pitch over a strongly inclined plane. The fall itself is not high, we believe only sixteen feet perpendicular, but its face is broken and irregular. Huge slabs of rock lie scattered below, in wild disorder. Some stand on their edges, leaning against the ledge from which they have been disunited. Some lie piled upon each other in the water, in inimitable confusion. A long, narrow island divides the fall nearly in the middle. Its eastern side is not perpendicular, but broken into three distinct leaps, below which the twisting and twirling eddies threaten destruction to any living thing that enters them. On the western side, in the boiling rapids below, a few rods from the fall, stands a little island, of a few yards area; rising steep from the waters, and covered with forest trees. At the time of our story, its mightiest oak was the haunt of a solitary bald eagle, that had built his eyrie on the topmost branches, beyond the reach of man. It was occupied by his posterity till the year eighteen hundred and twentythree, when the time honored crest of the vegetable monarch bowed and gave way before the wing of the northern tempest. The little islet was believed inaccessible, till two daring privates of the fifth regiment, at very low water, waded out in the river above, and ascending the fall by means of the blocks of stone before mentioned, forded the intervening space, and were the first of their species that ever set foot upon it.

Large trunks of trees frequently drift over, and diving into the chasms of the rocks, never appear again. The loon, or great northern diver, is also, at moulting time, when he is unable to rise from the water, often caught in the rapids. When he finds himself drawn in, he struggles with fate for a while, but finding escape impossible, he faces downwards and goes over, screaming horribly. These birds sometimes make the descent unhurt. Below, the rapids foam and roar and tumble for half a mile, and then subside into the clear, gentle current that continues unbroken to the Rock River Rapids; and at high water to the Gulf of Mexico. Here too, the high bluffs which enclose the Mississippi commence. Such was the scene at the time of this authentic history, but now it is mended or marred, according to the taste of the spectator, by the works of the sons of Adam. It can shew its buildings, its saw mill, its grist mill, its cattle, and its cultivated fields. Nor is it unadorned with traditional honors. A Siou can tell you how the enemy in the darkness of midnight, deceived by the false beacons lighted by his ancestors, paddled his canoe into the rapids, from which he never issued alive. He can give a good guess too, what ghosts haunt the spot, and what spirits abide there.

To return to our story: Toskatnay and his band passed the falls and raised their lodges a few rods above the rapids. It so happened that evening, that a violent quarrel arose between the two wives, which the presence of some of the elders only, prevented from ending in cuffing and scratching. When the master of the lodge returned, he rebuked them both, but the weight of his anger fell on Weenokhenchah Wandeeteekah, though in fact, the dispute had been fastened on her by the other. She replied nothing to his reproaches, but his words sunk deep into her bosom, for he had spoken scornfully of her, saying that no Siou had so pitiful a wife as himself. She sobbed herself to sleep, and when the word was given in the morning to rise and strike the tents, she was the first to rise and set about it.

While the business of embarkation was going on, it so chanced that the child of the poor woman crawled in the way of her rival, and received a severe kick from her. This was too much for the mother. Vociferating such terms as are current only at Billingsgate and in Indian camps, for squaws are not remarkable for delicacy of expression, she fastened upon the Heron's daughter tooth and nail, who was not slow to return the compliment. Luckily their knives were wrested from them by the bystanders, or one or both would have been killed on the spot. This done, the men laughed and the women screamed, but none offered to part them, till Toskatnay, who was busy at the other end of the camp, patching a

31

birch canoe, heard the noise, and came and separated them by main force. He was highly indignant at an occurrence that must bring ridicule upon him. The Heron's daughter he reproved, but Weenokhenchah Wandeeteekah he struck with his paddle repeatedly, and threatened to put her away. This filled the cup of her misery to overflowing: she looked at him indignantly and said, "You shall never reproach me again." She took up her child and moved away, but he, thinking it no more than an ordinary fit of sullenness, paid no attention to her motions.

His unkindness at this time had the effect of confirming a project that she had long revolved in her mind, and she hastened to put it in execution. She embarked in a canoe with her child, and pushing from the shore, entered the rapids before she was perceived. When she was seen, both men and women, among whom her husband was the most earnest, followed her on the shore, entreating her to land ere it was too late. The river was high, so that it was impossible to intercept her, yet Toskatnay, finding his entreaties of no avail, would have thrown himself into the water to reach the canoe, had he not been withheld by his followers. Had this demonstration of interest occurred the day before, it is possible that her purpose would have been forgotten. As it was, she shook her open hand at him in scorn, and held up his child for him to gaze at. She then began to sing, and her song ran thus.

"A cloud has come over me. My joys are turned to grief. Life has become a burden too heavy to bear, and it only remains to die.

"The Great Spirit calls, I hear his voice in the roaring waters. Soon, soon, shall they close over my head; and my song shall be heard no more.

"Turn thine eyes hither, proud chief. Thou art brave in battle, and all are silent when thou speakest in council. Thou hast met death, and hast not been afraid.

"Thou hast braved the knife, and the axe; and the shaft

of the enemy has passed harmless by thee.

"Thou hast seen the warrior fall. Thou hast heard him speak bitter words with his last breath.

"But hast thou ever seen him dare more than a woman is about to do?

"Many speak of thy deeds. Old and young echo thy praises. Thou art the star the young men look upon, and thy name shall be long heard in the land.

"But when men tell of thy exploits, they shall say, 'He slew his wife also!' Shame shall attend thy memory.

"I slew the ravenous beast that was about to destroy thee. I planted thy corn, and made thee garments and moccasins.

"When thou wast an hungred, I gave thee to eat, and when thou wast athirst, I brought thee cold water. I brought thee a son also, and I never disobeyed thy commands.

"And this is my reward! Thou hast laughed at me. Thou hast given me bitter words, and struck me heavy blows.

"Thou hast preferred another before me, and thou hast driven me to wish for the approach of death, as for the coming winter.

"My child, my child! Life is a scene of sorrow. I had not the love of a mother, did I not snatch thee from the woes thou must endure.

"Adorn thy wife with ornaments of white metal, Toskatnay. Hang beads about her neck. Be kind to her, and see if she will ever be to thee as I."

So saying, or rather singing, she went over the fall with her child, and they were seen no more.

One year precisely from this time, Toskatnay followed the track of a bear which he had wounded, to the brink of the falls. He halted opposite the spot where Weenokhenchah Wandeeteekah had disappeared, and gazed on the foaming rapid. What was passing in his mind it is impossible to say. He had reached the summit of his ambition. He was acknowledged a chief, and he had triumphed over the Beaver and the Chippeways. But her for whose sake he had spurned the sweetest flowers of life, true love and fond fidelity, had proved faithless to him, and fled to the Missouri with another man. He had nothing farther to look for, no higher eminence to attain, and his reflections were like those of him who wept because he had no more worlds to conquer. A strange occurrence roused him from his reverie. A snow white doe, followed by a fawn of the same color, came suddenly within the sphere of his vision; so suddenly, that they seemed to him to come out of the water. Such a sight had never before been seen by any of his tribe. He stood rooted to the ground. He who had never feared the face of man, trembled like an aspen with superstitious terror. The animals, regardless of his presence, advanced slowly towards him, and passed so near that he might have touched them with his gun. They ascended the bank and he lost sight of them. When they were fairly out of sight, he recovered from the shock, and stretching out his arms after them, conjured them to return. Finding his adjurations vain, he rushed up the bank, but could see nothing of them, which was the more remarkable that the prairie had just been burned over, and for a mile there was no wood or inequality in the ground, that could have concealed a much smaller animal than a deer.

He returned to his lodge, made a solemn feast, at which his relatives were assembled, and sung his death song. He told his wondering auditors that he had received a warning to prepare for his final change. He had seen the spirits of his wife and child. No one presumed to contradict his opinion. Whether founded in reason or not, it proved true in point of fact. Three weeks after, the camp was attacked by the Chippeways. They were repulsed, but Toskatnay, and he only, was killed.

No stone tells where he lies, nor can any of the Dahcotahs shew the spot. His deeds are forgotten, or at best, faintly remembered; thus showing "on what foundation stands the warrior's pride"; but his wife still lives in the memory of her people, who speak of her by the name of Weenokhenchah Wandeeteekah, or the Brave Woman.

Murnane and the *Illinois*

WILLIS GIBSON

A genius on a steamboat: that was Murnane. And not a man on the Union Line was there who didn't acknowledge it every day, and cheerfully.

Ten years he stood our Superintendent: a man stocky and sunburned, gentle-voiced and polite like a purser, and, as I said at the beginning, a genius. Deft as a poet he could recount the stories of the North Mississippi: of the Dakotahs, the Sacs, the Mormons, of Battle Island, and Nauvoo. And in the midst, perhaps, of Black Hawk's defeat, he could jump down to the main deck, where poets are not appreciated, and break up a roustabout mutiny faster than a company of Regulars. Many the ugly deckhand who noted the gentle voice failed to note the iron fist — until too late. He could scent a windstorm while the sky was yet empty; he could forge and set up an engine part better than any chief we had; he could give the steward pointers on desserts fit for the Planters' dining-room. Night and day he knew the river — twist, turn, bar, shallow — as though he, himself, had planned it. And these are surprising good points, every one. But, to my mind, the deed that, more than any other thing, stamped Murnane the man out of the ordinary was his run with the steamer *Illinois* in the Star-Union race. It was in the early days of Murnane's directorate that Captain Redford, a New Orleans navigator, came to the Upper River with the idea of revolutionizing things in the St. Louis-St. Paul trade: our trade. With him he brought the *Sultana,* a $75,000 side-wheel steamboat, new-built at Cincinnati, and three decrepit but brightly painted packets purchased at forced sale from a bankrupt Missouri River company.

Less than a month it took us to decide that the Star Line — the title Redford had given his enterprise — must go out of business, above St. Louis at least. Three years it took us to put the Star Line out, and even then we wouldn't have done it if it hadn't been for Murnane. More than that, we came so near to going out of business ourselves that for a good many hours we thought we were out.

Three years the boats of the Star Line and the boats of the Union Line steamed side by side on the Upper River, and waged a war, bitter as Homestead, crafty as the Mafia, stubborn as the Rebellion. Three years freights and passengers rode for half-rate, for quarter-rate, for nothing. Three years the directors of the Union Line, and Redford and his backers, dug deep into bank accounts and got nothing back.

Then opened the fourth season, as mean a squabble as ever. But in the first week a thing happened that was to change all: Redford made a fast trip with the *Sultana* from St. Paul to Dubuque, and gave the account to the Dubuque papers, claiming he had established a record. It was a fast trip, that of the *Sultana's,* and a worthy trip; for the St. Paul and Dubuque river holds as many bends to the mile as a corkscrew, and is none too roomy for a boat with 300 feet of bottom and a five-foot hold. But it wasn't the record, for, back in the seventies, the old Union Liner *Lincoln,* since broken up, had covered the course in a good two hours' less time. Kehoe, our president, nettled at Redford's claim, composed a long statement concerning the *Lincoln's* feat, and sent it into print. Redford, very hot, replied in an open letter so sarcastic that we held our breath when we read it. Kehoe wrote more letters, Redford wrote more. All sorts of river men, active and retired, contributed opinions; soon the papers from St. Louis to St. Paul were full of the controversy. And so ended the month of May, with Redford growing more boastful every hour.

On the first day of June Murnane strolled into Kehoe's office with a plan, a very simple plan, for stopping the dispute. Murnane talked an hour earnestly, and, when he had finished, Kehoe penned a challenge to Redford, worded something like this:

> To settle the question of speed supremacy over the so-called "Dubuque course," the steamer — — , representing the Star Line, and the steamer — — , representing the Union Line, will run a straightaway race from St. Paul, Minn., to Dubuque, Iowa, leaving St. Paul at 2 p.m. July 4th. The Mayor of St. Paul will start the race; the Mayor of Dubuque will judge the finish. Contesting steamers must be entered on or before July 3rd. No allowances will be made for delays of any sort; the first boat to tie up at Dubuque dock will be declared the winner.

This challenge Kehoe signed and mailed to Redford's office in St. Paul. Two days later it was back again, with Redford's name beneath Kehoe's.

Though the racers were not to be announced until July 3rd, it was well understood that the Star people would name the *Sultana,* and that we would name the *Iowa,* the sleek and chubby sprinter designed by Murnane and built at our own Dubuque yard.

As the June days passed the interest in the coming contest waxed warmer and warmer until there was little else talked of in the Valley. Bets were laid; small bets, and large. Kehoe wagered thousands; so did Redford.

And in the final week of the month Murnane went to Kehoe with another plan, not so simple this time.

"Kehoe," said he, "we've risked so much on this thing — money and reputation — why not risk a little more? I say, let the line that wins the race gain the exclusive right to the trade; let the line that loses lock its warehouses and agencies, and take its boats elsewhere forever."

Kehoe, certain the *Iowa* would win, was for it. Redford, certain the *Sultana* would win, was for it. And so an agreement was drawn and certified, and, after that, no further moves seemed possible, save the formal selecting of the candidates.

But on the morning of the twenty-fifth the *Iowa*, northbound, struck a snag at the head of Island 98 and sank. When the news sped north and south, Redford and his followers grinned; Kehoe and Murnane looked blank at each other. Murnane inspected the wreck next day and came away disheartened; he found the *Iowa* not fatally hurt, but impossible of raising for weeks. Hastily he looked over our other three boats, studied their records, and talked with their officers — and quit, still disheartened. Then, brightening, he dropped into Dubuque, spent the afternoon of the twenty-ninth there, and left at six-thirty for St. Louis.

The minute the train rolled into the shadow of the Union Depot, Murnane bolted for the office. He found Kehoe in and wasted no words in getting to business.

"Kehoe," declared Murnane, "I'm going to race the *Illinois*."

Kehoe laughed sorrowfully at his superintendent, and after, when he saw he was in earnest, he scoffed at him. For the *Illinois* was the veteran steamboat of the Union

Line: a side-wheeler, out of commission, and on the bank at the Dubuque yard five years, crowded out by boats newer, stancher, and more economical. In her day she had been a famous boat, and fast, but now — no wonder Kehoe scoffed.

"The old boat's a hulk, a shell, a junk heap," Kehoe wound up, "rusted, rotted, not even worth dismantling. When she first left the trade we advertised her, offered to give her away, almost; and nobody'd take her. Her hull wouldn't stand the current a half-day; her engines wouldn't hang together an hour. No, we'll have to take our chances with the *Chippewa,* the *Alton,* or the *Burlington* — they're good boats, aren't they?"

"Yes," replied Murnane calmly, "good boats — and slow boats. I don't know of any slower north of New Orleans. There's the *Chippewa.* You can jam steam into her boilers till you start the rivets, you can push her engines till the river's all foam for a mile astern — but you can't hurry her an inch beyond her everyday gait, and just so with the others. But the *Illinois* — I saw her yesterday — she's got some shape in her hull, and some style in her engines, and she's not so shaky as you think. I'll take charge of the *Illinois* myself, Kehoe; and, if I don't bring her first into Dubuque, you'll find us sunk or blown up somewhere on the course."

And Kehoe, who knew there was no brag in Murnane, consented, grumbling and doubtful.

Within an hour Murnane started back by train for Dubuque. Before daylight the first of July he set to work on the *Illinois,* the yard force aiding. He caulked her seams, braced her sides, and softened her machinery; he gave her a searchlight, and a plant to run it, and a steering engine — conveniences she had never owned before, — and by nightfall she was in the river, with a fresh certificate, cajoled from the inspectors somehow, in her cabin, and a picked crew on her decks: Hi Davis and Bill Owens, pilots; Gerry and Bell, chief engineers; Tim Burns, first mate; and a full crew of machinists, firemen, and roustabouts.

At midnight the *Alton* arrived from St. Louis on her regular trip, according to arrangement took the *Illinois* in tow, and went again on her northward way. Thus the old steamer journeyed slowly to St. Paul, and reached there, without mishap, at noon of the third. And then Murnane walked quickly to the city Hall, and there entered the steamer *Illinois,* John Murnane, Master, as the representative of the Union Line. And Redford, who had been awaiting him, entered the steamer *Sultana* as his choice, and elected to command her in person.

The afternoon of the Fourth came hot and clear at St. Paul, with the river at four feet and rising. The *Sultana,* as handsome a steamboat as man ever fashioned, gay with bunting, and sprinkled with invited guests, lay ready at the foot of Sibley Street — the post Redford had won for her in the morning's drawing for starting positions. The *Illinois,* gray and grimy, with not a speck of color save the crimson pennant of the line, noisy with hammering, and half hidden by the steam that sputtered from her leaky pipes, rocked at the foot of Jackson, a block above the *Sultana.* On her upper deck, three of us from the St. Louis office sat, the only passengers.

Sharp at two the Mayor of St. Paul nodded a signal. The *Sultana* cast off and wheeled lazily into the Bend; the *Illinois* switched and floundered after: the three-hundred-mile race for Dubuque was on. For the first two hours there was no excitement to it. The *Sultana* ahead simply loafed, scoring ten miles an hour. Owens, who had our first wheel trick, wanted to squeeze by her, and begged Murnane for the chance again and again, but the channel is narrow through the Minnesota meadows, and the *Sultana* was weaving all over it, besides tossing up a tricky swell, and Murnane wouldn't risk the try until we were in sight of Hastings, about half-past four. There he gave the word, and, while the *Sultana* fiddled in the west passage of Hastings drawbridge, Owens slipped the *Illinois* through the east passage, and led into the bluff country at a twelve-mile gait.

The joining of the St. Croix deepens the water from Hastings down, but the crookedness is worse, and crookedness was what the *Illinois* loved. And once among the bends, Billy Owens started in on some dainty steering, steering such as never had been seen before in those waters. At times he coaxed the rudder by ripple-widths, at times he drove the wheel down so fast the steering engine smoked in every bearing. He missed wingdams by inches only, on the turns he shaved the shore so close the branches brushed our stern. But not once did he reckon wrongly. Redford's pilots were nervy — he had two in the house after leaving Hastings bridge — they worked fast and took chances, but, with every curve and crossing finished, the *Sultana* fell away. At Diamond Bluff she was swallowed up in the winding cañon behind.

Six-thirty found us past Red Wing and close to the lake inlet. It is a great widening of the Mississippi: Lake Pepin — thirty miles from gate to gate, and deeper far than any sounding pole — a place grand and treacherous. It is a speedway where steamboat engines may be loosed at will, a beautiful basin where, in minutes, the gentle breeze of summer may change to a hurricane of death.

Even now we were worrying; since four there had been wind; and, as we pushed by the last point, a scowl sprang to the face of every man on lookout. For Pepin was rough: clear to the tiny blue hills about the outlet — mountains they are when you near them — a field of frothy white-caps twinkled in the lowering sun.

Free of the entrance channel, the *Illinois* wallowed in the choppy lake like a yawl in a seaway, but Hi Davis, who had taken the wheel at supper-time, after a fight pinned her nose on Maiden Rock, the first headmark, and called for a bit of extra speed, though the increase wasn't much, for Murnane didn't want to urge the worn machinery any more than he could help.

Meanwhile Murnane and the office squad gathered aft on the top deck to watch for the *Sultana*. We were out ten minutes, no more, when a white flash cleaved the green of the north shore and the Star Line racer sought the lake. Without a dip or quiver she came, the smoke curling heavy about her chimneys, the steam leaving her exhaust pipes in feathery darts. From the moment she rounded for the Rock she gained surely. Off Maiden Rock village but a scant mile danced between the boats; Murnane broke for the pilot-house.

"Full stroke on the engines, Hi," he snapped. "Stir up everybody below." The little whistle in the engine-room squealed "full stroke" instantly. Words for the machine men, irreverent but pointed, tumbled through the speaking tubes.

Another mile and the *Illinois,* every stick a-tremble, hull and structure heaving as though in earthquake's grasp, a sleet of live cinders trailing overhead, a wake of foam boiling astern, was splitting Pepin's green water like a torpedo boat on her trial trip. The roar of the draught in the chimneys, the harsh clank of crowded engines, the creaking of racked timber, the drum of paddles — every second we listened for a crash. But those engines and boilers and hull timbers stood up to the run like thoroughbreds. From Frontenac to Lake City, from Lake City to Read's Landing — through the ten-mile South End in thirty-seven minutes — the *Illinois* held her lead, and better, over the boat with the canoe hull and Cincinnati machinery.

The lake narrows and ends at Read's Landing; the Mississippi begins again. And a little distance below the outlet Chippewa Valley bridge, a pile structure with a pontoon draw, crosses from Minnesota to Wisconsin. It was eight o'clock — sunset-time — when we lined up joyously for this bridge, and then came the break we had dreaded: a cam yoke on the starboard engine sprang loose, and, in a twinkling, put a bad mess of rods and brackets about the cylinder, halting the *Illinois* fair in front of the landing. Murnane dropped an anchor over, and with the engineers, went at the trouble like lightning; and, while they tugged and hammered and straightened, the

Sultana, at first a black smudge back on the gilded lake, swiftly grew and grew, until, a vast white pile of power and motion, she swept splashing by us, through the bridge, and disappeared in the woods below.

They say bad luck runs in streaks, and I believe it. If it wasn't a streak we struck foul at Read's Landing, I don't know what it was. And the first thing to get mixed in it, after the cam yoke, was the Chippewa Valley bridge. I want to say, right here, a steamboat-man hates a draw-bridge. If a draw opens on a first whistle signal, he is astonished; if the draw, opened, stays in that pose long enough for him to sneak his boat through, he is astonished some more. You can't figure on a draw at all. And so, when, just as the pounding in the engine-room ceased, and Murnane loped for the anchor, Chippewa Valley bridge swung ponderously shut, we were not astonished, only grieved. The train that asked passage, a string of gravel-laden flats drawn by a toy engine, had crawled out on the trestle approach, unnoticed by us. 'Twas a worrisome wait while the little engine coughed, and toiled, and tugged at her flats; and a puzzle whether she'd ever get them across, so stubborn did they roll; but, in the end, steam and sand conquered; the draw opened; and the *Illinois* passed through.

Stalled our steamer had been for thirty minutes, and thirty minutes meant six miles to the rear. Murnane said she must make it up. Again the engineers unwound the throttles, and stared wistfully at steam-dial pointers fluttering fifty pounds beyond the lawful figure. At Alma the daylight had gone, but we had gained ten minutes — so said watchers at the landing; — at Minneiska ten more — the *Sultana's* searchlight flared in the southern sky; — then, beneath Mount Vernon, the fog, which had been in the air since sundown, settled over the river.

Navigation in a night fog is more than dangerous; there is but one rule for such weather: grope your steamboat to the nearest tree and tie up. But to-night it was different. Murnane and the *Illinois* weren't tying up for any fog, not to-night. Nor were Redford and the *Sultana*. The valley never knew a drearier fog — it hung on every hand solid and wet and cold and silent. The dusky bluffs, the landmarks of tree and rock, the yellow beacons — all were vanished. The searchlight shot out a useless white shaft of curling mist. In the quiet, the faint jingles for engines, the nervous peals for checking, shocked our ears like the clamor of fire bells. Drifting, we could even hear the oil sputtering on the hot pistons, the water dripping from the bucket planks. Mile after mile we stole through it, sounding every length, the wheel stirring slowly, often not at all. Sometimes a shift of the cloud would uncover a beacon, far away and faint like a firefly; then the pilots — Owens had gone up now to help Davis fight the fog — would exclaim "Lone Oak Light," or whatever light it was, and we'd plough for it full head — but never more than a minute was it before the speck was blotted out, and we'd go to drifting and sounding again.

All the while we counted to find the *Sultana* aground somewhere; for it seemed unreasonable that she could steer her great bulk safely through the vapor, but, though we kept sharp watch, we saw nought of her.

A little past midnight a clump of blurred red spots glimmered on the port side, and Murnane pronounced them the street arc lights of Fountain City. Because of an old-fogy notion of Kehoe's, Fountain City was our northern coal station. Because Kehoe, starting in the business twenty years before with a little La Crosse and Alma packet, had bought his coal at the City yard: so, now, it was the order for the Union Line steamers, southbound, instead of coaling at St. Paul or Dubuque, to take on a coal barge at the City and carry it alongside until the load was transferred. And to-night, of all unhandy nights, we had a coal barge to pick up at Fountain City. As we edged in toward the yard levee, Murnane looked sour enough. Not a sign of a lantern was there about the yard, but, after a time, Owens got the *Illinois* ranged abreast the barge mooring ground. We, up on the hurricane deck, blinded by the fog, could only listen for the clatter of Burns and his men coupling on the barge. But no clatter followed, and Murnane, impatient, called down, and asked Burns why he didn't make fast. Burns answered he couldn't see anything to make fast to. Murnane, thinking we were too far out, told Owens to work in slow. The *Illinois* sidled shoreward ten feet or less, and bumped heavily against something sunken — then we knew the bad luck was still with us. Torches, hurriedly brought, threw a feeble light over the slack water next the levee, and there we saw our coal barge heeled over on her side, with her coal spilled in the river to the last sweeping. Murnane was pretty mad, we could see that, but whether waves from a passing steamer had forced the barge against the levee piling and crushed in her side, or whether she had sunk from mere old age — both these accidents had happened previously at the City yard — he didn't take time to find out. He dropped the *Illinois* down to the main landing, and from there departed on a run for the depot to wire Winona and La Crosse for coal and barges for loading. Inside of ten minutes the answers were back — duplicates: "Plenty of coal but no barges."

Murnane came out of the depot and shouted the messages, and then disappointment surged thick all through the *Illinois*. The engineers threw down their oilers and settled, downcast, into chairs; the Negro firemen, weeping dismay, got ready to bank the fires; Burns began laying out some extra lines for the tying up and forgot to mix the bad words with the orders, so disgusted was he; Davis, who, though off watch, had been working with Owens at the wheel since midnight, started for his stateroom, and with him went every one else who was free to do so.

But it was all wrong. When Murnane sprang down the bank and across the stage, he didn't say anything about extra lines, and Burns told his helpers to quit; nor did he say anything about banking fires, nor going to bed.

Instead he came trotting up-stairs to the hurricane deck, and briskly tolled the three-tap "Ready" signal on the big bell. Burns, swearing gleefully, set a stampede going on the forecastle; the engineers jumped out of their chairs; the firemen grabbed their shovels; Davis clawed back up the pilot-house steps; those of us who had started for berths turned and ran pattering forward, chock-full of inquiry. As we gained the headrail beside Murnane, Bell, the chief engineer on watch, appeared on the forecastle beneath us.

"There ain't coal enough left to last us half an hour, Cap'n," he protested.

"There'r other things besides coal that'll burn," answered Murnane cheerfully. Before Bell could question further, Murnane pulled the "let go" stroke — BOOM — and shouted up at the pilots: "Go on down the river, boys."

There was a splashing of lines in the water, a rattle of engine bells, a hiss of steam, and, with everybody aboard wondering save Murnane, the *Illinois* once more headed south into the mist, with a handicap of twenty minutes to wipe out, according to figures given by the depot operator.

Murnane didn't keep us long in suspense. As soon as the steamer reached mid-river, he jogged down to the main deck, and presently returned with a file of deckhands, all carrying axes. Behind them marched a second detail carrying nothing, and, yet later, Burns. Murnane directing, the ax-men went to chopping down the texas — the upper cabin, as the landsman knows it — walls, roof, floor, berths, partitions; and as fast as the structure was torn away the axless men hurried it to the furnaces — all but the roof, which, being some tin, and some tar, and some gravel, wouldn't burn, and was dumped over the side.

When the work was well under way, Murnane left it with Burns, and explained his scheme.

"We're going to keep those fires hot," said he, "if we have to split this boat to kindling from texas to keelson. I

47

sha'n't be surprised if we go into Dubuque with nothing but the hull and machinery, and the pilot-house on the bow."

As Murnane had planned it, we crept along: now in the channel, now out; sometimes guided by a beacon, oftener by nothing, and, as we blundered on, the axmen hewed fuel out of the texas, and the helpers bore it below.

Two hours in the eight-mile stretch south of Fountain City brought us to Winona, and there we performed the hazardous trick of threading two drawbridges in the fog. From the engineer on the lower bridge we learned that the *Sultana* was not but seven minutes ahead.

Nevertheless, we didn't catch her for almost an hour; then, of a sudden, through a rift in the fog, she loomed square abreast, as big as a mountain, and not a light showing save her red and green chimney lanterns. Moving the faster, we slipped past her easily, but the minute we were by, she swung in behind us. And it was uncanny, somehow, those colored lanterns, floating back there in the gloom; for with the closing of the rift all else of the *Sultana* was hidden. Till a quarter to four she stuck at our stern, and then, in the neighborhood of Trempealeau shoals, she seemed to find trouble, for the lanterns slowly dimmed and finally faded out.

At four o'clock the fog began changing from black to gray, and, with the sunrise, from gray to white. By five the sun stood a pale pink disc well up in the east and the fog was turning restive. Two hours it lazily rose and fell, thinned and thickened, giving us hazy glimpses of the shore, and at seven, as we approached La Crosse, it rose and rolled away for good. Anxiously we looked up-river for the *Sultana*'s white shape, and no trace was there; but miles back, plain against the brilliant blue of the valley's horizon, hung a little puff of gray smoke.

And now began trouble with the fuel. While the axmen had had the light, flimsy texas, it had been easy, very easy, to keep the fires bright enough for the low pressure carried during the night. But with the going of the fog it was another proposition. From La Crosse the *Illinois* wanted a full head of steam, and under the forced draught the sun-baked wood flashed away in the furnaces like powder. And the texas was gone — all but a few posts left to support the pilot-house. Different the choppers found it below decks — they couldn't tear away woodwork right and left, for the removal of a principal timber, or the shifting of a truss, meant a sure collapse in the hull.

So slow was the finding of fuel that the fires waned often for the lack of it. In the first hour after leaving La Crosse the *Illinois* made eight miles, in the second hour eleven, in the third nine, her speed governed exactly by the supply of fuel. This way the morning wore along, the gray smoke back in the valley following steadily, and gradually overtaking us. Toward twelve o'clock the smoke began to gain rapidly, and by two in the afternoon it had grown very near and very black.

Faster flashed the axes through the boiler deck, through the main deck. Faster crumbled to firewood the long tinselled cabin, and the little faded staterooms, that in their time had heard the laughter of fair women, the whispers of politicians; that had seen the meetings of statesmen, the brawls of gamblers; that had sheltered men of war and peace, of order and disorder — the greatest and the basest souls of the new West.

Two hours we held the pace to thirteen miles and our advantage looked safe, but at four o'clock, off Cassville, with Dubuque but thirty miles away, Burns reported trouble below the water line. Murnane dived for the hold and found it afloat, with the river bubbling in through many splits in the sides and bottom. It was nothing to explain the leakage — the wrecking of the upper works had warped the hull and started the seams — and, for a little, 'twas nothing, with patches and a hose laid to the steam pump, to keep the water back. But, as the miles slipped by, the racking of the engines and the pressure of the river told on the weakened hull, and by and by the cracks began to open faster than we could count them, and the *Illinois* began to fall inch by inch.

Nearer moved the dogging smoke cloud. As we left Specht's Ferry it floated over the trees at the head of the four-mile reach astern, and out over the water; and, a minute after, the *Sultana* forged around the bend and into the reach.

Such was the finish of the Star-Union race: a fourteen-mile battle between a steamboat in the pink of trim and a waterlogged sinking skeleton. And how Murnane did urge on his racer! Under her hull he drew bandages and inside he built timber props; the steam pump he set thumping fast as a dynamo engine; the choppers and helpers — there was fuel enough by the boilers now to carry us through — he put to bailing with buckets. But still the *Illinois* settled, and her speed lessened from ten miles to eight miles — to six miles. Off Eagle Point, in sight of Dubuque, the *Sultana* had crept within seven or eight lengths. But the lead of the *Illinois* was enough to send her first through Dubuque drawbridge at a quarter to seven. Then she turned for Dubuque dock: the last thousand yards. Barely strength had she to meet the current pushing at her starboard side, the main deck amidships was awash: every minute it seemed she must go under.

But Murnane, perched way forward on the upper deck, was not a whit worried — in fact he was smiling a bit, for on the corner of the wharf we could make out Kehoe, crazily waving his arms and howling things we couldn't hear.

"Have your boys ready with the lines, Tim," Murnane called gently down to Burns. "They'd better hang tight on to something until you give the word." To the pilot, Davis: "Tell the engineer to have a handful of steam in reserve, Hi."

While Murnane talked the *Illinois* lay in the water sluggish as a dying creature. Fifty feet from the dock she lost headway and commenced sliding back with the current.

Murnane wheeled toward the pilot-house like a flash. "Now, Hi," he shouted. Davis, snatching fast at the bell ropes, sent a wild alarm to the engineers and screamed into the tube: "Now give it to her, *give* it to her." The engines answered with jar upon jar, the steamer hung still, then moved ahead again. The black river washed over the main deck and joined the river rising in the hatches. The *Illinois* lurched to port, feebly grazed Dubuque dock, and sank like lead in eight feet.

The decks were slanting like toboggan slides, the fire drowned, the engineers and the deck crew up to their necks, Davis fast in the pilot-house casings, and we St. Louis fellows hanging by our nails to the remnants of the cabin skylight; but Murnane, braced on a chimney guy, was as gravely watchful as though his steamboat was landing in a twenty-foot harbor with a stiff water foaming at the bow.

"Get out your head and stern lines, lively, Tim," he ordered. "I want a spring line too."

Burns's men, wet, but grinning, scrambled out of the river and ashore with the hawsers, and drew them taut on the mooring piles. "All solid, sir," sung Burns.

Murnane looked back to the *Sultana;* she was just emerging from the drawbridge. Turning again to the dock, he picked the Mayor of Dubuque in the crowd.

"Steamer *Illinois* is moored," said Murnane, solemn as a judge. "I believe the articles specify: 'The first boat to tie up.'"

"Correct," returned the Mayor, just as solemn.

Philo Gubb's Greatest Case

ELLIS PARKER BUTLER

Philo Gubb, wrapped in his bathrobe, went to the door of
the room that was the headquarters of his business of
paper-hanging and decorating as well as the office of his
detective business, and opened the door a crack. It was
still early in the morning, but Mr. Gubb was a modest
man, and, lest any one should see him in his scanty attire, he peered through the crack of the door before he
stepped hastily into the hall and captured his copy of the
Riverbank Daily Eagle. When he had secured the still
damp newspaper, he returned to his cot bed and spread
himself out to read comfortably.

It was a hot Iowa morning. Business was so slack that
if Mr. Gubb had not taken out his set of eight varieties of
false whiskers daily and brushed them carefully, the
moths would have been able to devour them at leisure.

P. Gubb opened the *Eagle*. The first words that met his
eye caused him to sit upright on his cot. At the top of the
first column of the first page were the headlines

MYSTERIOUS DEATH OF HENRY SMITZ
Body Found in Mississippi River by Boatman Early This A.M.
Foul Play Suspected.

Mr. Gubb unfolded the paper and read the item under the headlines with the most intense interest. Foul play meant the possibility of an opportunity to put to use once more the precepts of the Course of Twelve Lessons, and with them fresh in his mind Detective Gubb was eager to undertake the solution of any mystery the Riverbank could furnish. This was the article: —

> Just as we go to press we receive word through Policeman Michael O'Toole that the well-known mussel-dredger and boatman, Samuel Fliggis (Long Sam), while dredging for mussels last night just below the bridge, recovered the body of Henry Smitz, late of this place.
>
> Mr. Smitz had been missing for three days and his wife had been greatly worried. Mr. Brownson, of the Brownson Packing Company, by whom he was employed, admitted that Mr. Smitz had been missing for several days.
>
> The body was found sewed in a sack. Foul play is suspected.

"I should think foul play would be suspected," exclaimed Philo Gubb, "if a man was sewed into a bag and deposited into the Mississippi River until dead."

He propped the paper against the foot of the cot bed and was still reading when someone knocked on his door. He wrapped his bathrobe carefully about him and opened the door. A young woman with tear-dimmed eyes stood in the doorway.

"Mr. P. Gubb?" she asked. "I'm sorry to disturb you so early in the morning, Mr. Gubb, but I couldn't sleep all night. I came on a matter of business, as you might say. There's a couple of things I want you to do."

"Paper-hanging or deteckating?" asked P. Gubb.

"Both," said the young woman. "My name is Smitz —

53

Emily Smitz. My husband — ”

"I'm aware of the knowledge of your loss, ma'am," said the paper-hanger detective gently.

"Lots of people know of it," said Mrs. Smitz. "I guess everybody knows of it — I told the police to try to find Henry, so it is no secret. And I want you to come up as soon as you get dressed, and paper my bedroom."

Mr. Gubb looked at the young woman as if he thought she had gone insane under the burden of her woe.

"And then I want you to find Henry," she said, "because I've heard you can do so well in the detecting line."

Mr. Gubb suddenly realized that the poor creature did not yet know the full extent of her loss. He gazed down upon her with pity in his bird-like eyes.

"I know you'll think it strange," the young woman went on, "that I should ask you to paper a bedroom first, when my husband is lost; but if he is gone it is because I was a mean, stubborn thing. We never quarreled in our lives, Mr. Gubb, until I picked out the wall-paper for our bedroom, and Henry said parrots and birds-of-paradise and tropical flowers that were as big as umbrellas would look awful on our bedroom wall. So I said he hadn't anything but Low Dutch taste, and he got mad. 'All right, have it your own way,' he said, and I went and had Mr. Skaggs put the paper on the wall, and the next day Henry didn't come home at all.

"If I'd thought Henry would take it that way, I'd rather had the wall bare, Mr. Gubb. I've cried and cried, and last night I made up my mind it was all my fault and that when Henry came home he'd find a decent paper on the wall. I don't mind telling you, Mr. Gubb, that when the paper was on the wall it looked worse than it looked in the roll. It looked crazy."

"Yes'm," said Mr. Gubb, "it often does. But, however, there's something you'd ought to know right away about Henry."

The young woman stared wide-eyed at Mr. Gubb for a moment; she turned as white as her shirtwaist.

"Henry is dead!" she cried, and collapsed into Mr. Gubb's long, thin arms.

Mr. Gubb, the inert form of the young woman in his arms, glanced around with a startled gaze. He stood miserably, not knowing what to do, when suddenly he saw Policeman O'Toole coming toward him down the hall. Policeman O'Toole was leading by the arm a man whose wrists bore clanking handcuffs.

"What's this now?" asked the policeman none too gently, as he saw the bathrobed Mr. Gubb holding the fainting woman in his arms.

"I am exceedingly glad you have come," said Mr. Gubb. "The only meaning into it, is that this is Mrs. H. Smitz, widow-lady, fainted onto me against my will and wishes."

"I was only askin'," said Policeman O'Toole politely enough.

"You shouldn't ask such things until you're asked to ask," said Mr. Gubb.

After looking into Mr. Gubb's room to see that there was no easy means of escape, O'Toole pushed his prisoner into the room and took the limp form of Mrs. Smitz from Mr. Gubb, who entered the room and closed the door.

"I may as well say what I want to say right now," said the handcuffed man as soon as he was alone with Mr. Gubb. "I've heard of Detective Gubb, off and on, many a time, and as soon as I got into this trouble I said, 'Gubb's the man that can get me out if anyone can.' My name is Herman Wiggins."

"Glad to meet you," said Mr. Gubb, slipping his long legs into his trousers.

"And I give you my word for what it is worth," continued Mr. Wiggins, "that I'm as innocent of this crime as the babe unborn."

"What crime?" asked Mr. Gubb.

"Why, killing Hen Smitz — what crime did you think?" said Mr. Wiggins. "Do I look like a man that would go and murder a man just because — "

He hesitated and Mr. Gubb, who was slipping his suspenders over his bony shoulders, looked at Mr. Wiggins with keen eyes.

"Well, just because him and me had words in fun," said Mr. Wiggins. "I leave it to you, can't a man say words in fun once in a while?"

"Certainly sure," said Mr. Gubb.

"I guess so," said Mr. Wiggins. "Anybody'd know a man don't mean all he says. When I went and told Hen Smitz I'd murder him as sure as green apples grow on a tree, I was just fooling. But this fool policeman — "

"Mr. O'Toole?"

"Yes. They gave him this Hen Smitz case to look into, and the first thing he did was to arrest me for murder. Nervy, I call it."

Policeman O'Toole opened the door a crack and peeked in. Seeing Mr. Gubb well along in his dressing operations, he opened the door wider and assisted Mrs. Smitz to a chair. She was still limp, but she was a brave little woman and was trying to control her sobs.

"Through?" O'Toole asked Wiggins. "If you are, come along back to jail."

"Now, don't talk to me in that tone of voice," said Mr. Wiggins angrily. "No, I'm not through. You don't know how to treat a gentleman like a gentleman, and never did."

He turned to Mr. Gubb.

"The long and short of it is this: I'm arrested for the murder of Hen Smitz, and I didn't murder him and I want you to take my case and get me out of jail."

"Ah, stuff!" exclaimed O'Toole. "You murdered him and you know you did. What's the use talkin'?"

Mrs. Smitz leaned forward in her chair.

"Murdered Henry?" she cried. "He never murdered Henry. I murdered him."

"Now, ma'am," said O'Toole politely, "I hate to contradict a lady, but you never murdered him at all. This man here murdered him, and I've got the proof on him."

"I murdered him!" cried Mrs. Smitz again. "I drove him out of his right mind and made him kill himself."

"Nothing of the sort," declared O'Toole. "This man Wiggins murdered him."

"I did not!" exclaimed Mr. Wiggins indignantly. "Some other man did it."

It seemed a deadlock, for each was quite positive. Mr. Gubb looked from one to the other doubtfully.

"All right, take me back to jail," said Mr. Wiggins. "You look up the case, Mr. Gubb; that's all I came here for. Will you do it? Dig into it, hey?"

"I most certainly shall be glad to so do," said Mr. Gubb, "at the regular terms."

O'Toole led his prisoner away.

For a few minutes Mrs. Smitz sat silent, her hands clasped, staring at the floor. Then she looked up into Mr. Gubb's eyes.

"You will work on this case, Mr. Gubb, won't you?" she begged. "I have a little money — I'll give it all to have you do your best. It is cruel — cruel to have that poor man suffer under the charge of murder when I know so well Henry killed himself because I was cross with him. You can prove he killed himself — that it was my fault. You will?"

"The way the deteckative profession operates onto a case," said Mr. Gubb, "isn't to go to work to prove anything particularly especial. It finds a clue or clues and follows them to where they lead to. That I shall be willing to do."

"That is all I could ask," said Mrs. Smitz gratefully.

Arising from her seat with difficulty, she walked tremblingly to the door. Mr. Gubb assisted her down the stairs, and it was not until she was gone that he remembered that she did not know the body of her husband had been found — sewed in a sack and at the bottom of the river. Young husbands have been known to quarrel with their wives over matters as trivial as bedroom wallpaper; they have even been known to leave home for several days at a time when angry; in extreme cases they have even been known to seek death at their own hands; but it is not at all usual for a young husband to leave home for several days and then in cold blood sew himself in a sack and jump into the river. In the first place there are easier ways of terminating one's life; in the second place a man can jump into the river with perfect ease without going to the trouble of sewing himself in a sack; and in the third place it is exceedingly difficult for a man to sew himself into a sack. It is almost impossible.

To sew himself into a sack a man must have no little skill, and he must have a large, roomy sack. He takes, let us say, a sack-needle, threaded with a good length of twine; he steps into the sack and pulls it up over his head; he then reaches above his head, holding the mouth of the sack together with one hand while he sews with the other hand. In hot anger this would be quite impossible.

Philo Gubb thought of all this as he looked through his disguises, selecting one suitable for the work he had in hand. He had just decided that the most appropriate disguise would be "Number 13, Undertaker," and had picked up the close black wig, and long, drooping mustache, when he had another thought. Given a bag sufficiently loose to permit free motion of the hands and arms, and a man, even in hot anger, might sew himself in. A man, intent on suicidally bagging himself, would sew the mouth of the bag shut and would then cut a slit in the front of the bag large enough to crawl into. He would then crawl into the bag and sew up the slit, which would be immediately in front of his hands. It could be done! Philo Gubb chose from his wardrobe a black frock coat and a silk hat with a wide band of crape. He carefully locked his door and went down to the street.

On a day as hot as this day promised to be, a frock coat and a silk hat could be nothing but distressingly uncomfortable. Between his door and the corner, eight various citizens spoke to Philo Gubb, calling him by name. In fact, Riverbank was as accustomed to seeing P. Gubb in disguise as out of disguise, and while a few children might be interested by the sight of Detective Gubb in disguise, the older citizens thought no more of it, as a rule, than of seeing Banker Jennings appear in a pink shirt one day and a blue striped one the next. No one ever accused Banker Jennings of trying to hide his identity by a change of shirts, and no one imagined that P. Gubb was trying to disguise himself when he put on a disguise. They considered it a mere business custom, just as a butcher tied on a white apron before he went behind his counter.

This was why, instead of wondering who the tall, dark-garbed stranger might be, Banker Jennings greeted Philo Gubb cheerfully.

"Ah, Gubb!" he said. "So you are going to work on this Smitz case, are you? Glad of it, and wish you luck. Hope you place the crime on the right man and get him the full penalty. Let me tell you there's nothing in this rumor of Smitz being short of money. We did lend him money, but we never pressed him for it. We never even asked him for interest. I told him a dozen times he could have as much more from us as he wanted, within reason, whenever he wanted it, and that he could pay me when his invention was on the market."

"No report of news of any such rumor has as yet come to my hearing," said P. Gubb, "but since you mention it, I'll take it for less than it is worth."

"And that's less than nothing," said the banker. "Have you any clue?"

"I'm on my way to find one at the present moment of time," said Mr. Gubb.

"Well, let me give you a pointer," said the banker. "Get a line on Herman Wiggins or some of his crew, understand. Don't say I said a word, — I don't want to be brought into this, — but Smitz was afraid of Wiggins and his crew. He told me so. He said Wiggins had threatened to murder him."

"Mr. Wiggins is at present in the custody of the county

jail for killing H. Smitz with intent to murder him," said Mr. Gubb.

"Oh, then — then it's all settled," said the banker. "They've proved it on him. I thought they would. Well, I suppose you've got to do your little bit of detecting just the same. Got to air the camphor out of the false hair, eh?"

The banker waved a cheerful hand at P. Gubb and passed into his banking institution.

Detective Gubb, cordially greeted by his many friends and admirers, passed on down the main street, and by the time he reached the street that led to the river he was followed by a large and growing group intent on the pleasant occupation of watching a detective detect.

As Mr. Gubb walked toward the river, other citizens joined the group, but all kept a respectful distance behind him. When Mr. Gubb reached River Street and his false mustache fell off, the interest of the audience stopped short three paces behind him and stood until he had rescued the mustache and once more placed its wires in his nostrils. Then, when he moved forward again, they too moved forward. Never, perhaps, in the history of crime was a detective favored with a more respectful gallery.

On the edge of the river, Mr. Gubb found Long Sam Fliggis, the mussel dredger, seated on an empty tar-barrel with his own audience ranged before him listening while he told, for the fortieth time, the story of his finding of the body of H. Smitz. As Philo Gubb approached, Long Sam ceased speaking, and his audience and Mr. Gubb's gallery merged into one great circle which respectfully looked and listened while Mr. Gubb questioned the mussel dredger.

"Suicide?" said Long Sam scoffingly. "Why, he wan't no more a suicide than I am right now. He was murdered or wan't nothin'! I've dredged up some suicides in my day, and some of 'em had stones tied to 'em, to make sure they'd sink, and some thought they'd sink without no ballast, but nary one of 'em ever sewed himself into a bag, and I give my word," he said positively, "that Hen Smitz couldn't have sewed himself into that burlap bag unless someone done the sewing. Then the feller that did it was an assistant-suicide, and the way I look at it is that an assistant-suicide is jest the same as a murderer."

The crowd murmured approval, but Mr. Gubb held up his hand for silence.

"In certain kinds of burlap bags it is possibly probable a man could sew himself into it," said Mr. Gubb, and the crowd, seeing the logic of the remark, applauded gently but feelingly.

"You ain't seen the way he was sewed up," said Long Sam, "or you wouldn't talk like that."

"I haven't yet took a look," admitted Mr. Gubb, "but I aim so to do immediately after I find a clue onto which to work up my case. An A-1 deteckative can't set forth to work until he has a clue, that being a rule of the game."

"What kind of a clue was you lookin' for?" asked Long Sam. "What's a clue, anyway?"

"A clue," said P. Gubb, "is almost anything connected with the late lamented, but generally something that nobody but a deteckative would think had anything to do with anything whatsoever. Not infrequently often it is a button."

"Well, I've got no button except them that is sewed onto me," said Long Sam, "but if this here sack-needle will do any good — "

He brought from his pocket the point of a heavy sack-needle and laid it in Philo Gubb's palm. Mr. Gubb looked at it carefully. In the eye of the needle still remained a few inches of twine.

"I cut that off'n the burlap he was sewed up in," volunteered Long Sam. "I thought I'd keep it as a sort of nice little souvenir. I'd like it back again when you don't need it for a clue no more."

"Certainly sure," agreed Mr. Gubb, and he examined the needle carefully.

There are two kinds of sack-needles in general use. In

both, the point of the needle is curved to facilitate pushing it into and out of a closely filled sack; in both, the curved portion is somewhat flattened so that the thumb and finger may secure a firm grasp to pull the needle through; but in one style the eye is at the end of the shaft while in the other it is near the point. This needle was like neither; the eye was midway of the shaft; the needle was pointed at each end and the curved portions were not flattened. Mr. Gubb noticed another thing — the twine was not the ordinary loosely twisted hemp twine, but a hard, smooth cotton cord, like carpet warp.

"Thank you," said Mr. Gubb, "and now I will go elsewhere to investigate to a further extent, and it is not necessarily imperative that everybody should accompany along with me if they don't want to."

But everybody did want to, it seemed. Long Sam and his audience joined Mr. Gubb's gallery and, with a dozen or so newcomers, they followed Mr. Gubb at a decent distance as he walked toward the plant of the Brownson Packing Company, which stood on the riverbank some two blocks away.

It was here Henry Smitz had worked. Six or eight buildings of various sizes, the largest of which stood immediately on the river's edge, together with the "yards" or pens, all enclosed by a high board fence, constituted the plant of the packing company, and as Mr. Gubb appeared at the gate the watchman there stood aside to let him enter.

"Good-morning, Mr. Gubb," he said pleasantly. "I been sort of expecting you. Always right on the job when there's crime being done, ain't you? You'll find Merkel and Brill and Jokosky and the rest of Wiggins's crew in the main building, and I guess they'll tell you just what they told the police. They hate it, but what else can they say? It's the truth."

"What is the truth?" asked Mr. Gubb.

"That Wiggins was dead sore at Hen Smitz," said the watchman. "That Wiggins told Hen he'd do for him if he lost them their jobs like he said he would. That's the truth."

Mr. Gubb — his admiring followers were halted at the gate by the watchman — entered the large building and inquired his way to Mr. Wiggins's department. He found it on the side of the building toward the river and on the ground floor. On one side the vast room led into the refrigerating room of the company; on the other it opened upon a long but narrow dock that ran the width of the building.

Along the outer edge of the dock were tied two barges, and into these barges some of Wiggins's crew were dumping mutton — not legs of mutton but entire sheep, neatly sewed in burlap. The large room was the packing and shipping room, and the work of Wiggins's crew was that of sewing the slaughtered and refrigerated sheep carcasses in burlap for shipment. Bales of burlap stood against one wall; strands of hemp twine ready for the needle hung from pegs in the wall and the posts that supported the floor above. The contiguity of the refrigerating room gave the room a pleasantly cool atmosphere.

Mr. Gubb glanced sharply around. Here was the burlap, here were needles, here was twine. Yonder was the river into which Hen Smitz had been thrown. He glanced across the narrow dock at the blue river. As his eye returned he noticed one of the men carefully sweeping the dock with a broom — sweeping fragments of glass into the river. As the men in the room watched him curiously, Mr. Gubb picked up a piece of burlap and put it in his pocket, wrapped a strand of twine around his finger and pocketed the twine, examined the needles stuck in improvised needle-holders made by boring gimlet holes in the wall, and then walked to the dock and picked up one of the pieces of glass.

"Clues," he remarked, and gave his attention to the work of questioning the men.

Although manifestly reluctant, they honestly admitted that Wiggins had more than once threatened Hen

Smitz — that he hated Hen Smitz with the hatred of a man who has been threatened with the loss of his job. Mr. Gubb learned that Hen Smitz had been the foreman for the entire building — a sort of autocrat with, as Wiggins's crew informed him, an easy job. He had only to see that the crews in the building turned out more work this year than they did last year. "'Ficiency" had been his motto, they said, and they hated "'Ficiency."

Mr. Gubb's gallery was awaiting him at the gate, and its members were in a heated discussion as to what Mr. Gubb had been doing. They ceased at once when he appeared and fell in behind him as he walked away from the packing house and toward the undertaking establishment of Mr. Holworthy Bartman, on the main street. Here, joining the curious group already assembled, the gallery was forced to wait while Mr. Gubb entered. His task was an unpleasant but necessary one. He must visit the little "morgue" at the back of Mr. Bartman's establishment.

The body of poor Hen Smitz had not yet been removed from the bag in which it had been found, and it was to the bag Mr. Gubb gave his closest attention. The bag — in order that the body might be identified — had not been ripped, but had been cut, and not a stitch had been severed. It did not take Mr. Gubb a moment to see that Hen Smitz had not been sewed in a bag at all. He had been sewed in burlap — burlap "yard goods," to use a shopkeeper's term — and it was burlap identical with that used by Mr. Wiggins and his crew. It was no loose bag of burlap — but a close-fitting wrapping of burlap; a cocoon of burlap that had been drawn tight around the body, as burlap is drawn tight around the carcass of sheep for shipment, like a mummy's wrappings.

It would have been utterly impossible for Hen Smitz to have sewed himself into the casing, not only because it bound his arms tight to his sides, but because the burlap was lapped over and sewed from the outside. This, once and for all, ended the suicide theory. The question was:

Who was the murderer?

As Philo Gubb turned away from the bier, Undertaker Bartman entered the morgue.

"The crowd outside is getting impatient, Mr. Gubb," he said in his soft, undertakery voice. "It is getting on toward their lunch hour, and they want to crowd into my front office to find out what you've learned. I'm afraid they'll break my plate-glass windows, they're pushing so hard against them. I don't want to hurry you, but if you would go out and tell them Wiggins is the murderer they'll go away. Of course there's no doubt about Wiggins being the murderer, since he has admitted he asked the stock-keeper for the electric-light bulb."

"What bulb?" asked Philo Gubb.

"The electric-light bulb we found sewed inside this burlap when we sliced it open," said Bartman. "Matter of fact, we found it in Hen's hand. O'Toole took it for a clue and I guess it fixes the murder on Wiggins beyond all doubt. The stock-keeper says Wiggins got it from him."

"And what does Wiggins remark on that subject?" asked Mr. Gubb.

"Not a word," said Bartman. "His lawyer told him not to open his mouth, and he won't. Listen to that crowd out there!"

"I will attend to that crowd right presently," said P. Gubb, sternly. "What I should wish to know now is why Mister Wiggins went and sewed an electric-light bulb in with the corpse for."

"In the first place," said Mr. Bartman, "he didn't sew it in with any corpse, because Hen Smitz wasn't a corpse when he was sewed in that burlap, unless Wiggins drowned him first, for Dr. Mortimer says Hen Smitz died of drowning; and in the second place, if you had a live man to sew in burlap, and had to hold him while you sewed him, you'd be liable to sew anything in with him.

"My idea is that Wiggins and some of his crew jumped on Hen Smitz and threw him down, and some of them held him while the others sewed him in. My idea is that

Wiggins got that electric-light bulb to replace one that had burned out, and that he met Hen Smitz and had words with him, and they clinched, and Hen Smitz grabbed the bulb, and then the others came, and they sewed him into the burlap and dumped him into the river.

"So all you've got to do is to go out and tell that crowd that Wiggins did it and that you'll let them know who helped him as soon as you find out. And you better do it before they break my windows."

Detective Gubb turned and went out of the morgue. As he left the undertaker's establishment the crowd gave a slight cheer, but Mr. Gubb walked hurriedly toward the jail. He found Policeman O'Toole there and questioned him about the bulb; and O'Toole, proud to be the center of so large and interested a gathering of his fellow citizens, pulled the bulb from his pocket and handed it to Mr. Gubb, while he repeated in more detail the facts given by Mr. Bartman. Mr. Gubb looked at the bulb.

"I presume to suppose," he said, "that Mr. Wiggins asked the stock-keeper for a new bulb to replace one that was burned out?"

"You're right," said O'Toole. "Why?"

"For the reason that this bulb is a burned-out bulb," said Mr. Gubb.

And so it was. The inner surface of the bulb was darkened slightly, and the filament of carbon was severed. O'Toole took the bulb and examined it curiously.

"That's odd, ain't it?" he said.

"It might seem so to the non-deteckative mind," said Mr. Gubb, "but to the deteckative mind, nothing is odd."

"No, no, this ain't so odd, either," said O'Toole, "for whether Hen Smitz grabbed the bulb before Wiggins changed the new one for the old one, or after he changed it, don't make so much difference, when you come to think of it."

"To the deteckative mind," said Mr. Gubb, "it makes the difference that this ain't the bulb you thought it was, and hence consequently it ain't the bulb Mister Wiggins got from the stock-keeper."

Mr. Gubb started away. The crowd followed him. He did not go in search of the original bulb at once. He returned first to his room, where he changed his undertaker disguise for Number Six, that of a blue woolen-shirted laboring-man with a long brown beard. Then he led the way back to the packing house.

Again the crowd was halted at the gate, but again P. Gubb passed inside, and he found the stock-keeper eating his luncheon out of a tin pail. The stock-keeper was perfectly willing to talk.

"It was like this," said the stock-keeper. "We've been working overtime in some departments down here, and Wiggins and his crew had to work overtime the night Hen Smitz was murdered. Hen and Wiggins was at outs, or anyway I heard Hen tell Wiggins he'd better be hunting another job because he wouldn't have this one long, and Wiggins told Hen that if he lost his job he'd murder him — Wiggins would murder Hen, that is. I didn't think it was much of anything but loose talk at the time. But Hen was working overtime too. He'd been working nights up in that little room of his on the second floor for quite some time, and this night Wiggins come to me and he says Hen had asked him for a fresh thirty-two-candle-power bulb. So I give it to Wiggins, and then I went home. And, come to find out, Wiggins sewed that bulb up with Hen."

"Perhaps maybe you have sack-needles like this into your stock-room," said P. Gubb, producing the needle Long Sam had given him. The stock-keeper took the needle and examined it carefully.

"Never had any like that," he said.

"Now, if," said Philo Gubb, — "if the bulb that was sewed up into the burlap with Henry Smitz wasn't a new bulb, and if Mr. Wiggins had given the new bulb to Henry, and if Henry had changed the new bulb for an old one, where would he have changed it at?"

"Up in his room, where he was always tinkering at that machine of his," said the stock-keeper.

"Could I have the pleasure of taking a look into that there room for a moment of time?" asked Mr. Gubb.

The stock-keeper arose, returned the remnants of his luncheon to his dinner-pail, and led the way up the stairs. He opened the door of the room Henry Smitz had used as a work-room, and P. Gubb walked in. The room was in some confusion, but, except in one or two particulars, no more than a work-room is apt to be. A rather cumbrous machine — the invention on which Henry Smitz had been working — stood as the murdered man had left it, all its levers, wheels, arms, and cogs intact. A chair, tipped over, lay on the floor. A roll of burlap stood on a roller by the machine. Looking up, Mr. Gubb saw, on the ceiling, the lighting fixture of the room, and in it was a clean, shining thirty-two-candle-power bulb. Where another similar bulb might have been in the other socket was a plug from which an insulated wire, evidently to furnish power, ran to the small motor connected with the machine on which Henry Smitz had been working.

The stock-keeper was the first to speak.

"Hello!" he said. "Somebody broke that window!" And it was true. Somebody had not only broken the window, but had broken every pane and the sash itself. But Mr. Gubb was not interested in this. He was gazing at the electric bulb and thinking of Part Two, Lesson Six of the Course of Twelve Lessons — "How to Identify by Finger-Prints, with General Remarks on the Bertillon System." He looked about for some means of reaching the bulb above his head. His eye lit on the fallen chair. By placing the chair upright and placing one foot on the frame of Henry Smitz's machine and the other on the chair-back, he could reach the bulb. He righted the chair and stepped onto its seat. He put one foot on the frame of Henry Smitz's machine; very carefully he put the other foot on

the top of the chair-back. He reached upward and un-
screwed the bulb.

The stock-keeper saw the chair totter. He sprang forward to steady it, but he was too late. Philo Gubb, grasp-
ing the air, fell on the broad, level board that formed the
middle part of Henry Smitz's machine.

The effect was instantaneous. The cogs and wheels of
the machine began to revolve rapidly. Two strong, steel
arms flopped down and held Detective Gubb to the table,
clamping his arms to his side. The roll of burlap unrolled,
and as it unrolled, the loose end was seized and slipped
under Mr. Gubb and wrapped around him and drawn
taut, bundling him as a sheep's carcass is bundled. An
arm reached down and back and forth, with a sewing motion, and passed from Mr. Gubb's head to his feet. As it
reached his feet a knife sliced the burlap in which he was
wrapped from the burlap on the roll.

And then a most surprising thing happened. As if the
board on which he lay had been a catapult, it suddenly
and unexpectedly raised Philo Gubb and tossed him
through the open window. The stock-keeper heard a
muffled scream and then a great splash, but when he ran
to the window, the great paper-hanger detective had disappeared in the bosom of the Mississippi.

Like Henry Smitz he had tried to reach the ceiling by
standing on the chair-back; like Henry Smitz he had
fallen upon the newly invented burlaping and loading
machine; like Henry Smitz he had been wrapped and
thrown through the window into the river; but, unlike
Henry Smitz, he had not been sewn into the burlap, because Philo Gubb had the double-pointed shuttle-action
needle in his pocket.

Page Seventeen of Lesson Eleven of the Rising Sun Detective Agency's Correspondence School of Detecting's
Course of Twelve Lessons says: —

In cases of extreme difficulty of solution it is well for the
detective to re-enact as nearly as possible the probable action of the crime.

Mr. Philo Gubb had done so. He had also proved that a man may be sewn in a sack and drowned in a river without committing willful suicide or being the victim of foul play.

Putting a Black-Leg on Shore

BENJAMIN DRAKE

A numerous and peculiar race of *modern* gentlemen may be found in the valley of the Mississippi. A naturalist would probably describe them as a genus of bipeds, gregarious, amphibious, and migratory. They seldom travel "solitary and alone"; are equally at home on land or water; and like certain vultures, spend most of their winters in Mississippi and Louisiana, their summers in the higher latitudes of Kentucky and Ohio. They dress with taste and elegance; carry gold chronometers in their pockets; and swear with the most genteel precision. They are supposed to entertain an especial abhorrence of the prevailing *temperance* fanaticism; and, as a matter of conscience, enter a daily protest against it, by sipping "mint-julaps" before breakfast, "hail-storms" at dinner, and "old Monongahela" at night. These gentlemen, moreover, are strong advocates of the race-path and the cock-pit; and, with a benevolence which they hold to be truly commendable, patronise modest merit, by playing *chaperon* to those wealthy young men who set out on the pilgrimage of life before they have been fully initiated into its pleasures. Every where throughout the valley, these mistletoe gentry are called by the original, if not altogether classic, cognomen of "Black-legs." The history of this euphonious epithet, or the reason of its application to so distinguished a variety of humanity, is unknown. The subject is one of considerable interest, and worthy the early attention of the Historical Society, to which it is respectfully commended.

It was the fortune of the steam-boat *Sea Serpent* of Cincinnati, commanded by Captain Snake, on her return from New Orleans in the spring of 1837, to number among her cabin passengers several highly respectable Black-Legs. One of them, Major Marshall Montgomery, a native of the "Old Dominion," belonged to the "Paul Clifford" school; and indeed, had, for some years past, borne testimony to the merit of Mr. Bulwer's romances, by making the hero of one of them his great prototype. In stature, the Major was over six feet, muscular, and finely proportioned. His taste in dress was only surpassed by the courtliness of his manners, and the ready flow of his conversation. In what campaign he had won the laurels that gave him his military title is unknown. It has been conjectured that the warlike prefix to his name may have resulted from the luxuriant brace of black whiskers which garnished his cheeks.

On a certain day, after dinner, the ladies having retired to their cabin for a *siesta,* the gentlemen, as usual, sat down to cards, chess, and back-gammon. The boat had just "wooded," and was nobly breasting the current of the river at the rate of eight knots an hour. Captain Snake, having nothing else to do, was fain to join in a rubber of whist; and it so happened that he and the Major were seated at the same table. This game, at the suggestion of Major Montgomery, was soon changed to "loo"; and played with varying success until at length, a pool of considerable magnitude had accumulated. As the contest for

72

the increasing stake advanced, much interest was excited among the by-standers, and still more in the players, with the exception of the Major, whose staid expression of countenance was a subject of general remark. He seemed careless about the run of the cards, and threw them, as if quite regardless of the tempting spoil that lay before him. At length the game was terminated. The fickle goddess disclosed her preference for the Major, by permitting him to win the "pool," amounting to near three hundred dollars. His success produced no outward signs of joy; he seemed, indeed, almost sorry to be compelled to take the money of his friends; and with much composure of manner, proposed to continue the play; making, at the same time, a very polite tender of his purse, to any gentleman at the table who might need a temporary loan.

In the group of spectators, there was a tall, spindle-legged young fellow from the Western Reserve, in Ohio, who had been to the South with a lot of cheese, for the manufacture of which that thriving New England colony is becoming quite famous. This cheese-monger had been watching the game from the beginning, and at last, fixing his eyes upon the winning Major, said, in a low, solemn tone of voice, suited to a more lugubrious subject,

"Well, now, that's right down slick, any how."

The Major, looking up, found the gaze of the company turned upon him. Knitting his brows he said, sternly, in reply,

"Let's have no more of your Yankee impertinence."

"Now, Mister," continued Jonathan in his drawling tone and with provoking coolness of manner, "you hadn't ought to let them there little speckled paste-boards play hide and go seek in your coat sleeve."

This remark, accompanied with a knowing wink of the speaker's eye, instantly transformed the Major into a young earthquake. Springing upon his feet, as if bent on blood and carnage, he bawled out at the top of his voice,

"Do you mean to insinuate, you Yankee pedlar — you

infernal wooden-nutmeg, that I have cheated?"

The young cheese merchant, leisurely rolling a huge cud of tobacco from one cheek to the other, and looking the Major steadfastly in the eye, replied with imperturbable gravity,

"Why you're the beatomest shakes I ever seed: who insinevated that you cheated? I didn't, no how: but if you don't behave a little genteeler, I conclude I'll tell as how I seed you slip a card under your sleeve, when you won that everlasting big pond of money."

"You are a liar," thundered the Major, in a perfect whirlwind, at the same time attempting to bring his bamboo in contact with the shoulders of his antagonist; but Jonathan caught the descending cane in his left hand; and, in turn, planted his dexter fist, with considerable impulse, on the lower end of the Major's breast bone, remarking,

"I say Mister, make yourself skerse there, or you'll run right against the end of my arm."

Unfortunately for the reputation of Major Montgomery, at this moment, a card fell from his coat sleeve; and with it fell his courage, for he turned suddenly round to the table to secure the spoils of victory. The Captain, however, had saved him the trouble, having himself taken up the money, for the purpose of returning it to those to whom it rightfully belonged. The Major, finding that his winnings and his reputation were both departing, became once more highly excited, and uttered direful anathemas against those who might dare to question his honour.

It is, perhaps, generally known to the reader, that the captain of a steam boat on the western waters is of necessity almost as despotic as the Grand Turk. The safety of his boat, and the comfort of his passengers, in performing a long and perilous trip, require, indeed, that such should be the case. Between port and port, he is sometimes called to act in the triple capacity of legislator, judge, and executioner. It is rumored, perhaps without any foundation, that in cases of great emergency, more than one of these commanders have seriously threatened a resort to the salutory influence of the "second section." Be this as it may, travellers on our western boats will consult their comfort and safety, by deporting themselves according to the gentlemanly principle. We throw out this hint for the public generally; and, in the fulness of our benevolence, commend it to the especial notice of tourists from the "fast anchored Isle."

Captain Snake made no reply to the imprecations of the Major, having far too much respect for his official station to permit himself to be drawn into personal conflict with one of his passengers. Stepping to the cabin door, his clear shrill voice was heard above the din of the Major's volcanic burst of passion and the loud whiz of the *Sea Serpent.* Instantly the tinkle of the pilot's bell responded to the order of his commander, and the boat lay-to, near the lee shore. Again the Captain's voice was heard,

"Jack! man the yawl; Major Montgomery wishes to go on shore."

"Aye, aye, Sir."

The Major looked round in utter astonishment. — The Captain again called out,

"Steward! put Major Montgomery's trunk in the yawl; he wishes to go on shore!"

"Aye, aye, Sir!"

The Major turned towards the Captain with a face indicating a mingled feeling of anger and dismay. — He had seen too much of life in the West, not to understand the fate that awaited him. Before he could make up his mind as to the best mode of warding off the impending catastrophe, Jack bawled out, "The yawl is ready, sir," and the steward cried, "The trunk is on board, sir."

Captain Snake bowed formally, and with a courteous, but singularly emphatic manner, said:

"Major Montgomery, the yawl waits."

The Major, however, retained his position near the card-table, and began to remonstrate against such very exceptionable treatment of a Virginia gentleman, whose character had never been questioned. He concluded by a broad intimation that on their arrival at Cincinnati, he should hold the captain personally responsible under the laws of honor. In reply, the captain of the *Sea Serpent* bowed again most profoundly, and turning toward the door of the cabin, said, calmly,

"Steward, call the Fireman to assist Major Montgomery into the yawl; he wishes to go on shore."

The redoubtable Major, in the vain hope that the passengers would sustain him in the contest, now threw himself on his reserved rights, ran up the flag of nullification, and ferociously brandished his Bowie knife: at this moment the Fireman made his appearance. He was a full-grown Kentuckian, born on the cedar knobs of the Blue Licks, and raised on sulphur water, pone, and 'possum fat. — Like many of his countrymen, he was an aspiring fellow, for he stood six-feet-four in his moccasins, and exhibited corresponding developments of bone and muscle. Hatless and coatless, with naked arms, and a face blackened with smoke and ashes, he might have passed for one of old Vulcan's journeymen, who had been forging thunderbolts for Jupiter, in some *regio-infernalis*. He stalked carelessly up to the bellicose Major, and before the latter was aware of it, seized the hand that held the upraised knife, and wrenched it away from him. The next instant the Major found himself fairly within the brawny arms of his antagonist. He struggled stoutly to extricate his elegant person from such an unwelcome embrace, but in vain. The fireman, displeased with the restless disposition of his captive, gave him one of those warm fraternal hugs which an old bear is wont to bestow upon an unmannerly dog that may venture to annoy his retreat from a farmer's hog-pen. This loving squeeze so completely mollified the rebellious feelings of the Major, that he suffered himself to be passively led into the yawl. The Captain's shrill voice was again heard,

"Pull away, my boys, Major Montgomery wishes to go on shore."

The oars dipped into the water and the yawl glided quickly to the beach. The afternoon was cloudy and dark; a drizzling rain was falling; the cotton-wood trees wore a funeral aspect; no vestige of a human habitation could be seen upon either shore, and the turbid waters of the Mississippi were hastening onwards, as if to escape from such a gloomy place.

Many of the passengers supposed that after the Major had been disgraced by being set on shore, he would be suffered to return; but those who entertained this opinion knew very little of the character of Captain Snake. That Major Montgomery should be a black-leg, was in his estimation no very heinous affair; for he held that in this republican country, and this democratic age, every man has a natural and inalienable right to choose his own occupation: But after having been permitted to play "loo" with the Captain of the fast running *Sea Serpent,* that the Major should slip a card, and then, lubberly rascal, be caught at it, — this was too bad, — absolutely unpardonable: There was something so vulgar, so very unprofessional in such conduct, that it was not to be tolerated.

The yawl touched the shore and was hastily disburthened of its trunk. The Major, however, after rising on his feet, looked wistfully back upon the *Sea Serpent,* and manifested no disposition to take refuge in a canebrake: Whereupon the Captain, becoming impatient, cried out,

"Fireman, lend a hand to assist Major Montgomery on shore."

The huge Kentuckian now began to approach the Major, who, having no particular relish for another fraternal hug, sprung to the beach, and sunk to his knees in mud. Thinking forbearance no longer a virtue, he poured out on the Captain a torrent of abuse: and, with wrathful oaths, threatened to publish him and his ugly, snail creeping steamer, from Olean Point to the alligator swamps of the Balize. The Captain made no reply, but the fireman, roused by hearing such opprobrious terms applied to his beloved *Sea Serpent,* called out in a voice, that was echoed from shore to shore,

"I say, Mr. Jack-of-knaves, it looks rather wolfy in these parts."

"Shut your black mouth, you scoundrel," retorted the Major, boiling over with rage.

"I say stranger," continued the fireman with provoking good humor, "would you swap them buffalo robes on your cheeks for a pair of 'coon-skins'?"

The Major stooped down for a stone to hurl at his annoying foe, but alas, he stood in a bed of mortar, and had no resource but that of firing another volley of curses.

"Halloo! my hearty," rejoined the fireman, "when you want to be rowed up 'salt river' again just tip me the wink; and remember Mr. King-of-Clubs, don't holler till you get out of the woods, or you'll frighten all the varmints."

During this colloquy, the young cheese-merchant stood on the guards of the boat, a silent spectator; but at length, as if suddenly shocked by the dreadful profanity of the Major, he raised his voice and bawled out,

"I say Mister, if you was away down east, I guess 'squire Dagget would fine you ever so much, for swearing so wicked; — that's the how."

The pilot's bell tinkled, the wheels resumed their gyrations, and again the majestic *Sea Serpent*

"Walked the waters like a thing of life."

Jonathan, with a look in which the solemn and comic were curiously blended, turned his eyes first towards the Captain, then upon the Major, and exclaimed,

"Well now the way these 'ere steam captains do things, is nothing to no body, no how."

And thus terminated one of those little episodes in the drama of life, not uncommon on the western Waters.

Maud Island

ERSKINE CALDWELL

Uncle Marvin was worried. He got up from the log and walked toward the river.

"I don't like the looks of it, boys," he said, whipping off his hat and wiping his forehead.

The houseboat was drifting downstream at about three miles an hour, and a man in a straw hat and sleeveless undershirt was trying to pole it inshore. The man was wearing cotton pants that had faded from dark brown to light tan.

"It looks bad," Uncle Marvin said, turning to Jim and me. "I don't like the looks of it one whit."

"Maybe they are lost, Uncle Marvin," Jim said. "Maybe they'll just stop to find out where they are, and then go on away again."

"I don't believe it, son," he said, shaking his head and wiping the perspiration from his face. "It looks downright bad to me. That kind of a houseboat never has been out for no good since I can remember."

On a short clothesline that stretched along the starboard side, six or seven pieces of clothing hung waving in the breeze.

"It looks awful bad, son," he said again, looking down at me.

We walked across the mud flat to the river and waited to see what the houseboat was going to do. Uncle Marvin took out his plug and cut off a chew of tobacco with his hackknife. The boat was swinging inshore, and the man with the pole was trying to beach it before the current cut in and carried them back to mid-channel. There was a power launch lying on its side near the stern, and on the launch was a towline that had been used for upstream going.

When the houseboat was two or three lengths from the shore, Uncle Marvin shouted at the man poling it.

"What's your name, and what do you want here?" he said gruffly, trying to scare the man away from the island.

Instead of answering, the man tossed a rope to us. Jim picked it up and started pulling, but Uncle Marvin told him to drop it. Jim dropped it, and the middle of the rope sank into the yellow water.

"What did you throw my rope in for?" the man on the houseboat shouted. "What's the matter with you?"

Uncle Marvin spat some tobacco juice and glared right back at him. The houseboat was ready to run on the beach.

"My name's Graham," the man said. "What's yours?"

"None of your business," Uncle Marvin shouted. "Get that raft away from here."

The houseboat began to beach. Graham dropped the pole on the deck and ran and jumped on the mud flat. He called to somebody inside while he was pulling the rope out of the water.

The stern swung around in the backwash of the current, and Jim grabbed my arm and pointed at the dim lettering on the boat. It said *Mary Jane,* and under that was *St. Louis.*

While we stood watching the man pull in the rope, two girls came out on the deck and looked at us. They were very young. Neither of them looked to be over eighteen or nineteen. When they saw Uncle Marvin, they waved at him and began picking up the boxes and bundles to carry off.

"You can't land that shantyboat on this island," Uncle Marvin said threateningly. "It won't do you no good to unload that stuff, because you'll only have to carry it all back again. No shantyboat's going to tie up on this island."

One of the girls leaned over the rail and looked at Uncle Marvin.

"Do you own this island, Captain?" she asked him.

Uncle Marvin was no river captain. He did not even look like one. He was the kind of man you could see plowing cotton on the steep hillsides beyond Reelfoot Lake. Uncle Marvin glanced at Jim and me for a moment, kicking at a gnarled root on the ground, and looked at the girl again.

"No," he said, pretending to be angry with her. "I don't own it, and I wouldn't claim ownership of anything on the Mississippi, this side of the bluffs."

The other girl came to the rail and leaned over, smiling at Uncle Marvin.

"Hiding out, Captain?" she asked.

Uncle Marvin acted as though he would have had something to say to her if Jim and I had not been there to overhear him. He shook his head at the girl.

Graham began carrying off the boxes and bundles. Both Jim and I wished to help him so we would have a chance to go on board the houseboat, but we knew Uncle Marvin would never let us do that. The boat had been beached on the mud flat, and Graham had tied it up, knotting the rope around a young cypress tree.

When he had finished, he came over to us and held out his hand to Uncle Marvin. Uncle Marvin looked at Graham's hand, but he would not shake with him.

"My name's Harry Graham," he said. "I'm from up the river at Caruthersville. What's your name?"

"Hutchins," Uncle Marvin said, looking him straight in the eyes, "and I ain't hiding out."

The two girls, the dark one and the light one, were carrying their stuff across the island to the other side where the slough was. The island was only two or three hundred feet wide, but it was nearly half a mile long. It had been a sandbar to begin with, but it was already crowded with trees and bushes. The Mississippi was on the western side, and on the eastern side there was a slough that looked bottomless. The bluffs of the Tennessee shore were only half a mile in that direction.

"We're just on a little trip over the weekend," Graham said. "The girls thought they would like to come down the river and camp out on an island for a couple of days."

"Which one is your wife?" Uncle Marvin asked him.

Graham looked at Uncle Marvin a little surprised for a minute. After that he laughed a little, and began kicking the ground with the toe of his shoe.

"I didn't quite catch what you said," he told Uncle Marvin.

"I said, which one is your wife?"

"Well, to tell the truth, neither of them. They're just good friends of mine, and we thought it would be a nice trip down the river and back for a couple of days. That's how it is."

"They're old enough to get married," Uncle Marvin told him, nodding at the girls.

"Maybe so," Graham said. "Come on over and I'll introduce you to them. They're Evansville girls, both of them. I used to work in Indiana, and I met them up there. That's where I got this houseboat. I already had the launch."

Uncle Marvin looked at the lettering on the *Mary Jane,* spelling out *St. Louis* to himself.

"Just a little fun for the weekend," Graham said, smiling. "The girls like the river."

Uncle Marvin looked at Jim and me, jerking his head

to one side and trying to tell us to go away. We walked down to the edge of the water where the *Mary Jane* was tied up, but we could still hear what they were saying. After a while, Uncle Marvin shook hands with Graham and started along up the shore towards our skiff.

"Come on, son, you and Milt," he said. "It's time to look at that trotline again."

We caught up with Uncle Marvin, and all of us got into the skiff, and Jim and I set the oarlocks. Uncle Marvin turned around so he could watch the people behind us on the island. Graham was carrying the heavy boxes to a clearing, and the two girls were unrolling the bundles and spreading them on the ground to air.

Jim and I rowed to the mouth of the creek and pulled alongside the trotline. Uncle Marvin got out his box of bait and began lifting the hooks and taking off catfish. Every time he found a hook with a catch, he took the cat off, spat over his left shoulder, and dropped it into the bucket and put on a new bait.

There was not much of a catch on the line that morning. After we had rowed across, almost to the current in the middle of the creek mouth, where the outward end of the line had been fastened to a cypress in the water, Uncle Marvin threw the rest of the bait overboard and told us to turn around and row back to Maud Island.

Uncle Marvin was a preacher. Sometimes he preached in the schoolhouse near home, and sometimes he preached in a dwelling. He had never been ordained, and he had never studied for the ministry, and he was not a member of any church. However, he believed in preaching, and he never let his lack of training stop him from delivering a sermon whenever a likely chance offered itself. Back home on the mainland, people called him Preacher Marvin, not so much for the fact that he was a preacher, but because he looked like one. That was one reason why he had begun preaching at the start. People had got into the habit of calling him Preacher Marvin, and before he was forty he had taken up the ministry as a calling. He had never been much of a farmer, anyway — a lot of people said that.

Our camp on Maud Island was the only one on the river for ten or fifteen miles. The island was only half a mile from shore, where we lived in Tennessee, and Uncle Marvin brought us out to spend the weekend five or six times during the summer. When we went back and forth between the mainland and the island, we had to make a wide circle, nearly two miles out of the way, in order to keep clear of the slough. The slough was a mass of yellow mud, rotting trees, and whatever drift happened to get caught in it. It was almost impossible to get through it, either on foot or in a flat-bottomed boat, and we kept away from it as far as possible. Sometimes mules and cows started out in it from the mainland to reach the island, but they never got very far before they dropped out of sight. The slough sucked them down and closed over them like quicksand.

Maud Island was a fine place to camp, though. It was the highest ground along the river for ten or fifteen miles, and there was hardly any danger of its being flooded when the high water covered everything else within sight. When the river rose to forty feet, however, the island, like everything else in all directions, was covered with water from the Tennessee bluffs to the Missouri highlands, seven or eight miles apart.

When we got back from baiting the trotline, Uncle Marvin told us to build a good fire while he was cleaning the catch of catfish and cutting them up for frying. Jim went off after an armful of driftwood while I was blowing the coals in the campfire. Jim brought the wood and built the fire, and I watched the pail of water hanging over it until Uncle Marvin was ready to make the coffee.

In the middle of the afternoon Uncle Marvin woke up from his midday nap and said it was too hot to sleep any longer. We sat around for ten or fifteen minutes, nobody saying much, and after a while Uncle Marvin got up and said he thought he would walk over to the other camp and see how the people from Caruthersville, or Evans-ville, or wherever they came from, were getting along.

Jim and I were up and ready to go along, but he shook his head and told us to stay there. We could not help feel-ing that there was something unusual about that, be-cause Uncle Marvin had always taken us with him no matter where he went when we were camping on the is-land. When Jim said something about going along, Uncle Marvin got excited and told us to do as he said, or we would find ourselves being sorry.

"You boys stay here and take it easy," he said. "I've got to find out what kind of people they are before we start in to mix with them. They're from up the river, and there's no telling what they're like till I get to know them. You boys just stay here and take it easy till I get back."

After he had gone, we got up and picked our way through the dry underbrush toward the other camp. Jim kept urging me to hurry so we would not miss seeing any-thing, but I was afraid we would make so much noise Uncle Marvin would hear us and run back and catch us looking.

"Uncle Marvin didn't tell them he's a preacher," Jim said. "Those girls think he's a river captain, and I'll bet he wants them to keep on thinking so."

"He doesn't look like a river captain. He looks like a preacher. Those girls were just saying that for fun."

"The dark one acted like she's foolish about Uncle Marvin," Jim said. "I could tell."

"That's Jean," I said.

"How do you know what their names are?"

"Didn't you hear Graham talking to them when they were carrying their stuff off that houseboat?"

"Maybe he did," Jim said.

"He called that one Jean, and the light one Marge."

Jim bent down and looked through the bushes.

"Uncle Marvin's not mad at them now for coming here to camp," he said.

"How can you tell he's not?" I asked Jim.

"I can tell by the way he's acting up now."

"He told Graham to get the houseboat away from here, didn't he?"

"Sure he did then," Jim whispered, "but that was before those two girls came outside and leaned over the railing and talked to him. After he saw them a while he didn't try to stop Graham from landing, did he?"

We had crawled as close as we dared go, and fifty feet away we could see everything that was going on in Graham's camp. When Uncle Marvin walked up, Graham was sitting against the trunk of a cypress trying to untangle a fishing line, and the two girls were lying in hammocks that had been hung up between trees. We could not see either of them very well then, because the sides of the hammocks hid them, but the sun was shining down into the clearing and it was easy to see them when they moved or raised their arms.

Five or six cases of drinks were stacked up against one of the trees where the hammocks were, and several bottles had already been opened and tossed aside empty. Graham had a bottle of beer beside him on the ground, and every once in a while he stopped tussling with the tangled fishing line and grabbed the bottle and took several swallows from it. The dark girl, Jean, had a bottle in her hand, half full, and Marge was juggling an empty bottle in the air over her head. Everybody looked as if he was having the best time of his life.

None of them saw Uncle Marvin when he got to the clearing. Graham was busy fooling with the tangled fishing line, and Uncle Marvin stopped and looked at all three of them for almost a minute before he was noticed.

"I'll bet Uncle Marvin takes a bottle," Jim said. "What do you bet?"

"Preachers don't drink beer, do they?"

"Uncle Marvin will, I'll bet anything," Jim said. "You know Uncle Marvin."

Just then Graham raised his head from the line and saw Uncle Marvin standing not ten feet away. Graham jumped up and said something to Uncle Marvin. It was funny to watch them, because Uncle Marvin was not looking at Graham at all. His head was turned in the other direction all the time, and he was looking where the girls lay stretched out in the hammocks. He could not take his eyes off them long enough to glance at Graham. Graham kept on saying something, but Uncle Marvin acted as though he was on the other side of the river beyond earshot.

Jean and Marge pulled the sides of the hammocks over them, but they could not make Uncle Marvin stop looking at them. He started to grin, but he turned red in the face instead.

Graham picked up a bottle and offered it to Uncle Marvin. He took it without even looking at it once, and held it out in front of him as if he did not know he had it in his hand. When Graham saw that he was not making any effort to open it, he took it and put the cap between his teeth and popped it off as easily as he could have done it with a bottle opener.

The beer began to foam then, and Uncle Marvin shoved the neck of the bottle into his mouth and turned it upside down. The foam that had run out on his hand before he could get the bottle into his mouth was dripping down his shirt front and making a dark streak on the blue cloth.

Jean leaned out of her hammock and reached to the ground for another bottle. She popped off the cap with a bottle opener and lay down again.

"Did you see that, Milt?" Jim whispered, squeezing my arm. He whistled a little between his teeth.

"I saw a lot!" I said.

"I didn't know girls ever did like that where everybody could see them," he said.

"They're from up the river," I told him. "Graham said they were from Evansville."

"That don't make any difference," Jim said, shaking his head. "They're girls, aren't they? Well, whoever saw girls lie in hammocks naked like that? I know I never did before!"

"I sure never saw any like those before, either," I told him.

Uncle Marvin had gone to the tree at the foot of one of the hammocks, and he was standing there, leaning against it a little, with the empty bottle in his hand, and looking straight at them.

Graham was trying to talk to him, but Uncle Marvin would not pay attention to what Graham was trying to say. Jean had turned loose the sides of the hammock, and Marge, too, and they were laughing and trying to make Uncle Marvin say something. Uncle Marvin's mouth was hanging open, but his face was not red any more.

"Why doesn't he tell them he's a preacher?" I asked Jim, nudging him with my elbow.

"Maybe he will after a while," Jim said, standing on his toes and trying to see better through the undergrowth.

"It looks to me like he's not going to tell them," I said. "It wouldn't make any difference, anyway, because Uncle Marvin isn't a real preacher. He only preaches when he feels like doing it."

"That doesn't make any difference," Jim said.

"Why doesn't it?"

"It just doesn't, that's why."

"But he calls himself a preacher, just the same."

"He doesn't have to be a preacher now if he doesn't want to be one. If he told them he was a preacher, they'd all jump up and run and hide from him."

Uncle Marvin was still standing against the tree looking at the dark girl, and Graham was a little to one side of him, looking as if he didn't know what to do next.

Presently Uncle Marvin jerked himself erect and turned his head in all directions listening for sounds. He looked towards us, but he could not see us. Jim got down on his hands and knees to be out of sight, and I got behind him.

The three others were laughing and talking, but not Uncle Marvin. He looked at them a while longer, and then he reached down to the top case against the cypress and lifted out another bottle. Graham reached to open it for him, but Uncle Marvin bit his teeth over the cap and popped it off. The beer began to foam right away, but before much of it could run out, Uncle Marvin had turned it up and was drinking it down.

When the bottle was empty, he wiped his mouth with the back of his hand and took three or four steps towards the dark girl in the hammock. Jean kicked her feet into the air and pulled the sides of the hammock around her. The other girl sat up to watch Uncle Marvin.

All at once he stopped and looked towards our camp on the other side of the island. There was not a sound anywhere, except the sucking sound in the slough that went on all the time, and the sharp slap of water against the sides of the houseboat. He listened for another moment, cocking his head like a dog getting ready to jump a rabbit, and broke into a run, headed for our camp. Jim and I just barely got there before Uncle Marvin. We were both puffing and blowing after running so fast, but Uncle Marvin was blowing even harder and he did not notice how short our breath was. He stopped and looked down at the dead fire for a while before he spoke to us.

"Get ready to go home, son, you and Jim," he said. "We've got to leave right now."

He started throwing our stuff into a pile and stamping out the ashes at the same time. He turned around and spat some tobacco juice on the live coals and grabbed up an armful of stuff. He did not wait for us to help him, but started for our skiff on the mud flat right away with a big load of stuff in both arms. Jim and I had to hurry to catch up with him so he would not forget and leave us behind.

He took the oars from us and shoved off without waiting for us to do it for him. When we were out of the mouth of the creek, he took his hat off and threw it on the bottom of the skiff and bent over the oars harder than ever. Jim and I could not do a thing to help, because there were only two oars and he would not turn either one of them loose.

Nobody said a thing while we were rowing around the slough. When we got within a hundred feet of shore, Uncle Marvin started throwing our stuff into a heap in the stern. We had no more than dragged bottom on shore when he picked up the whole lot and threw the stuff on the dried mud. The pans and buckets rolled in every direction.

Both of us were scared to say a word to Uncle Marvin because he had never acted like that before. We stood still and watched him while he shoved off into the river and turned the skiff around and headed around the slough. We were scared to death for a while, because we had never seen anybody cut across so close to the slough. He knew where he was all the time, but he did not seem to care how many chances he took of being sucked down into the slough. The last we saw of him was when he went out of sight around Maud Island.

We picked up our things and started running with them towards home. All the way there we were in too much of a hurry to say anything to each other. It was about a mile and a half home, and upgrade every step of the way, but we ran the whole distance, carrying our heavy stuff on our backs.

When we reached the front gate, Aunt Sophie ran out on the porch to meet us. She had seen us running up the road from the river, and she was surprised to see us back home so soon. When we left with Uncle Marvin early that morning, we thought we were going to stay a week on Maud Island. Aunt Sophie looked down the road to see if she could see anything of Uncle Marvin.

Jim dropped his load of stuff and sank down on the porch steps panting and blowing.

"Where's your Uncle Marvin, Milton?" Aunt Sophie asked us, standing above me and looking down at us with her hands on her hips. "Where's Marvin Hutchins?"

I shook my head the first thing, because I did not know what to say.

"Where's your Uncle Marvin, James?" she asked Jim.

Jim looked at me, and then down again at the steps. He tried to keep Aunt Sophie's eyes from looking straight into his.

Aunt Sophie came between us and shook Jim by the shoulder. She shook him until his hair tumbled over his face, and his teeth rattled until they sounded as if they were loose in his mouth.

"Where is your Uncle Marvin, Milton?" she demanded, coming to me and shaking me worse than she had Jim. "Answer me this minute, Milton!"

When I saw how close she was to me, I jumped up and ran out into the yard out of her reach. I knew how hard she could shake when she wanted to. It was lots worse than getting a whipping with a peach-tree switch.

"Has that good-for-nothing scamp gone and taken up with a shantyboat wench again?" she said, running back and forth between Jim and me.

I had never heard Aunt Sophie talk like that before, and I was so scared I could not make myself say a word. I had never heard her call Uncle Marvin anything like that before, either. As a rule she never paid much attention to him, except when she wanted him to chop some stovewood, or something like that.

Jim sat up and looked at Aunt Sophie. I could see that he was getting ready to say something about the way she talked about Uncle Marvin. Jim was always taking up for him whenever Aunt Sophie started in on him.

Jim opened his mouth to say something, but the words never came out.

"One of you is going to answer me!" Aunt Sophie said. "I'll give you one more chance to talk, Milton."

"He didn't say where he was going or what he was going to do, Aunt Sophie. Honest, he didn't!"

"Milton Hutchins!" she said, stamping her foot.

"Honest, Aunt Sophie!" I said. "Maybe he went off somewhere to preach."

"Preach, my foot!" she cried, jamming her hands on her hips. "Preach! If that good-for-nothing scalawag preached half as many sermons as he makes out like he does, he'd have the whole country saved for God long before now! Preach! Huh! Preach, my foot! That's his excuse for going off from home whenever he gets the notion to cut-up-jack, but he never fools me. And I can make a mighty good guess where he is this very minute, too. He's gone chasing off after some shantyboat wench! Preach, my foot!"

Jim looked at me, and I looked at Jim. To save our life we could not see how Aunt Sophie had found out about the two girls from Evansville on Maud Island.

Aunt Sophie jammed her hands on her hips a little harder and motioned to us with her head. We followed her into the house.

"We're going to have a house cleaning around this place," she said. "James, you bring the brooms. Milton, you go start a fire under the washpot in the back yard and heat it full of water. When you get it going good, come in here and sweep down the cobwebs off the ceilings."

Aunt Sophie went from room to room, slamming doors behind her. She began ripping curtains down from the windows and pulling the rugs from the floor. A little later we could hear the swish of her broom, and presently a dense cloud of dust began blowing through the windows.

Ram Him, Damn Him!

H. BEDFORD-JONES

Haikes drew in between two store fronts and once more read the letter before destroying it. That letter had come by some spy messenger through the Union lines. Here in New Albany, on the Indiana shore, it had reached him. He scanned it briefly:

> Fleet of Federal rams, reconstructed steamboats — rendezvous at New Albany. Understand they need pilots. Might be worth your while — bring flagship into our lines — permanent position, good pay, assured you in Confederate service —
>
> Geo. Montgomery,
> Conf. River Defense Flotilla.

An old friend, George Montgomery, the only one who had stood up for him. That had been two years ago, before the war.

Haikes tore up the paper, fed it into his mouth in

scraps, and swallowed it. He felt better when it was gone; that paper had an unpleasant smell of hemp about it. He walked on to the corner, and the scrawled placard tacked up there caught his eye. He paused, to squint with somber black eyes as the words leaped for him in the spring sunshine:

STEAMBOAT MEN WANTED FOR A TRIP DOWNRIVER. COL. CHARLES ELLET.

Steamboat men, eh? That ruffled his bitter thoughts. Uncle Sam could use steamboat men now, after having set the best of them ashore before war broke! Owen Haikes, first-class river pilot, spat his contempt for the placard, and turned to survey the levee.

The smoking, belching stacks of a half score steamboats lying against the shore, with the Ohio current tugging at their low hulls, held his interest. The New Albany levee did not often stage a show of this kind. Haikes paced up and down, hulking, raw-boned; all the sartorial glory of a river pilot had long since been shed. He was shabby.

Get a pilot's job, eh? Might be done, in emergencies like this; there might or might not be any registration lists handy; in war time you could get away with anything. Papers didn't count, only performance. Get a pilot's job and turn over the craft to the Confederates, eh? Damn old George, anyhow!

"I don't love the government, Lord knows," thought Haikes. "But do it for hire, for Confederate gold? Be damned to the lot of 'em! A soldier might do that, a captain or an engineer or a mate might do it — but damned if a master pilot would do it!"

To look at him, it was hard to conceive that he had, not so long ago, been that proudest, highest paid of all river men — a master pilot. But a second look would note something keen and resolute and steady in the eye, a sudden strength in the mouth and chin, a hard, masterful personality. Owen Haikes might be broken in fortune and future, but the man in him had not been touched.

He eyed the river craft shrewdly. Nine steam craft, two coal barges. Two side-wheel packets; *Queen of the West,* and *Monarch,* of the Cairo-Cincinnati run. He knew them well. A small side-wheeler, *Lancaster;* a dumpy stern-wheeler, *Switzerland.* Three tow-boats, *Mingo, Samson,* and *Lioness;* and two little pilot-boats or tenders.

His hungry eyes devoured the *Queen.* Why, she had been like a mother to him! He had been cub pilot aboard her, knew every inch of her. Now what the devil had they done to her and to the *Monarch?* Low and heavy in the water, she rode like a barge, instead of a packet designed for speed, easy handling, and scant draught. Pilot house planked up to the ledge panels, rails of hurricane and boiler decks planked up; bow built forward until it jutted like a long, sharp nose. A fighting ship now, a ram.

Haikes edged his way into the groups of curious spectators, kept back from the gang-planks by a few armed guards. He listened to the comments from all around.

"They must be going to run the blockade with supplies, eh?"

"Down the Mississipp'? Like hell! They ain't got no guns — them two big side-wheelers are floating barns! The Rebel gunboats will blow 'em sky-high. Who's this Colonel Ellet?"

There was a laugh and a snicker.

"Ain't you heard? Why, he's a bridge engineer; that's the closest to the water he ever got. A fine commodore for a fleet! You know what he's set out to do? I hear he aims to ram a way with these here wooden boats through the iron-plated gunboats, past the land forts, and on to join up with Farragut at New Orleans! If that ain't crazy, what is?"

"Yeah, he's been advertising for river men — steamboat men, he calls 'em — to serve as volunteers. By hickory, I wouldn't be in ary engine room or pilot-house of them floating barns for a thousand dollars gold!"

"Shucks! The Rebels have rams, too, and gunboats, and first class pilots. Remember Jack Hughes? He hailed from Louisville when he was on the lower Ohio run. He's down there. I heard tell."

Haikes suddenly wakened, and turned thundercloud eyes to the speaker. "What's that you said? Jackson Hughes — what's he doing?"

"Piloting for the Johnny Rebs. He joined up with 'em a year ago. Hey! here comes the colonel now. Got a telegram, but he ain't got his pilot, I bet."

A slight, stooped, agile man in blue frock coat and colonel's shoulder straps, an eager light on his thinly smooth face, was hastening down the levee, the paper of a telegram fluttering in his hand. Haikes strode out and overtook him at the gangplank of the *Queen*.

"Colonel Ellet?"

"Yes, sir?" The blue eyes were tired but bright with impatience. The long nose twitched nervously; a weary smile touched the large mouth. "What is it?"

"I hear you want river men."

"I did. Now I want only a chief pilot, but I can likely pick one up at Cairo. If not, I'll stand at the wheel myself. I've no time to lose."

"Which boat needs a pilot?" asked Haikes. The blue eyes appraised him.

"The *Queen*, the flagship; she shows the way. Must have a good pilot for her."

"How'll you get her to Cairo without a pilot?"

"I've a Louisville rapids tow-boat man who knows the river."

"A tow-boat pilot on the *Queen*, a big side-wheeler?" The voice of Haikes rasped with unconscious authority. "Where are you bound, out of Cairo?"

Colonel Ellet threw back his head and spoke tartly.

"To destroy the Confederate fleet at Memphis. Who are you, sir?"

"You're talking to a river man. You say you'd take the *Queen* down yourself? Do you know the wheel, do you know the river? It takes a pilot for a big craft like that. Why, you'd wreck her in no time!"

"I can follow the *Monarch* until we sight the enemy — "

"And a hell of a course you'd hold," snapped Haikes. "Let's go aboard. I'd like to have a word with you."

"Very well. Make it short. I'm under orders and we're fired up; but come along."

He briskly led the way past the guards with carbines at the present, up the gang-plank to the main deck, up the companionway to the boiler deck and hurricane deck, and on to his own stateroom forward in the texas, beneath the pilot-house perched on the roof. Haikes, who would know the way blindfolded, followed impatiently.

Once in the cabin, Colonel Ellet turned.

"Well? Out with it."

"My name's Smith, Tom Smith," said Haikes harshly. "I'm a top notch pilot, sir. I'm on shore at present and ready for a job. I'll pilot the *Queen* to Memphis for you."

The other grunted. "You have a license — a full master pilot?"

"I'm recorded, yes." Haikes did not say his name had been removed from the registry; that name of his might have been spotted. "I've no papers with me, but what's the difference? Performance counts; anyone could forge papers who had a mind. I know this boat, I earned my license on her. I know the wheel and the river, from Pittsburgh to New Orleans. This boat will burn five hundred cords of wood between St. Louis and New Orleans, Colonel. That's the practical sort of information you'll need to have."

Ellet, he saw at once, knew nothing of river life. Any river man would have asked more questions as to past service and present standing, but Ellet seemed to take any ragged stranger for granted. Perhaps he took the stranger's resolute eye and manner for granted. He frowned and gestured to a seat.

"Sit down. You say you know this boat?"

"I can take her through waters where the catfish are rigged with stern wheels. I was raised aboard her. She's cranky, and her pilot must know her well."

"If you sign on with my command, do you know what you're getting into?"

"Yes and no. I haven't read the news."

"There's been no news, except local rumors, of this expedition." Ellet paused, and Haikes suppressed the smile that came to his lips. No news, eh? But George Montgomery and the rebels had full news. "I was given twenty days to find my boats and refit them as rams; my own idea. The Confederates have steamboat rams; I've improved on them. We're going down to Memphis with Commodore Foote's ironclad gunboats from St. Louis. We're assigned to destroy the Confederate rams while our gunboats fight the rebel gunboats."

"Packet against packet, and pilot against pilot, eh?"

"Exactly. And ram against ram. We have no guns, merely a small force of volunteer sharpshooters to stand off boarders; we're to depend on ramming. Stem to stem, my man. I may lose boats, but they and the enemy boats will go down together."

"What's the matter with using Foote's ironclads alone, sir?"

"The steamboats are too fast for them." Ellet tapped the paper in his hand. "Here are the details of what's happened. The gunboat fleet made a try below Cairo. Two were rammed and sunk above Fort Pillow; the rest put back and left the Confederates to take station. We're casting off at once; the other boats follow as soon as possible. If you have nerve enough to ram or be rammed, you can take the wheel at Cairo; until then, Brazee will have charge."

Ram or be rammed! Suddenly Haikes felt cold; around him was the shudder and give of collapsing timbers, the awful feel of a stoved boat. Whether by his own fault or another's, the spasm of a piled-up boat beneath his feet was something a pilot could never forget.

All the agony of the *Scott* came back upon him full force — that stranded hulk just awash, and the wrecked *General Scott,* that lost him his license and future, made him a marked man on the river, a doomed man.

"The *Queen's* timbers won't stand for ramming," he said, dry-mouthed.

"I'm a construction engineer; we've braced hull and decks with timbers run fore and aft, beam to beam, with bulkheads in the hull forward. We've built the timber braces out beyond the bows, for her ram beak." Colonel Ellet stepped to the door. "You can serve in the engine-room down to Cairo."

"No, I won't; not me!" broke out Haikes. "I'll be up on watch. She'll be crankier than ever, with that nose and extra weight. I'll not have her wrecked under me ahead of time. When it comes to ramming — well, if they catch her broadside on, she'll go like an eggshell!"

His tone, his words, drew appreciation rather than rebuke. Ellet nodded, and left the cabin, pausing for a last word over his shoulder.

"Doesn't matter; our job is to clear the river. Do as you please. You've a few minutes to look around before we're off."

Haikes, left alone, cursed softly under his breath and went over the boat with grim appraisal. Once trim and spick and span, the old *Queen of the West* was a sight now. Her fancy rails were turned into timbered bulwarks. She was braced under the decks, the engine room was a planked fort. That damned timber ram, faced with boiler iron! She was heavy in the water, low by the bows, and would handle like a scow. At the first shock she would lose her stacks —

Lose her stacks! Haikes thought of the *General Scott,*

and cold sweat started on his forehead. Her stacks had toppled; one had swayed for the pilot-house; his own life had nearly been snuffed out. Those immensely tall iron stacks that carried spouting flame high in air were destroying angels when they went over. Here were blue-coats with new Springfield carbines and six-shooter revolvers, lounging in the cabin, on the boiler deck and main deck. A gabble of talk was everywhere. Another Ellet, younger brother of the colonel and captain in the Illinois volunteers, commanded these "river marines," with headquarters on the *Monarch*. The talk rose high. The colonel was over fifty. He was no soldier, but a civilian engineer who built bridges; he could not deliver a military order. His brother, made a lieutenant-colonel for this job, was about as river-wise as a hen on a hencoop in a freshet. At the thought of taking orders from landsmen, Haikes cursed afresh.

He stumped up to the hurricane deck, on up the ladder to the Texas roof and the barricaded pilot-house. A slim young fellow was here, leaning against the wheel and chomping with nervous jaws at his quid — a sure sign that he did not fancy his job. This must be the Louisville man, Brazee; now handling a boat bigger than his measure, and a sidewheeler to boot. He flung a stare and curt greeting at Haikes.

"Who are you? You can't stay in this house."

"I'm the pilot. Taking her over at Cairo."

Haikes bid savagely for the worst, and paused. There was no stiffening of body, no shaming retort. His face meant nothing to the stripling.

"Well, you're right welcome to her." The young fellow spat over the window ledge. "I'll run the rapids at low water, but I'll not stand up here to be rammed, not for Luke Brazee! You heard what was done to those ironclads? The Johnnies in their paddle steamers tore right through 'em."

"Colonel Ellet just told me," Haikes took the seat under the window.

"You're a Lower Mississip' pilot?"

"So I've heard."

Haikes smiled grimly. To be aboard the *Queen* once more — why, he was a new man! Already his lie to Ellet was justified, in his own heart. To reveal his actual story would have meant a curt rejection, would have ruined his chance.

And here, he perceived clearly and resolutely, the great chance was offered him; not to redeem himself, for he was guiltless of any fault, but to rise above destiny. The irony of it! Montgomery fancied he was so far broken and done for as to play traitor — Haikes spat at the very thought, then smiled again. Sooner or later he must tell Colonel Ellet the whole truth. By then, performance would justify him. Ellet was no soldier, and in this very fact he found fresh springing hope; the man wanted a job done, not technicalities and red tape.

Haikes looked over at the *Monarch,* but could not make out who was at the wheel in her pilot-house. Colonel Ellet, with boyish enthusiasm, went running forward on the hurricane deck; with drawn sword he struck the bell framed forward of the stacks, then hopped to the shore rail and his voice rang out.

"Cast off!"

By the squeal of hoisting tackle, the gang-plank was being lifted. The lines were cast off the snubbing posts. The young fellow spun the wheel, and with a jerk of the wooden-handled cord gave the backing bell.

The exhaust pipes puffed. The *Queen* trembled as her paddles threshed. The crowd ashore cheered. She backed out and cleared; working ahead and aback with her paddles, she swung her stern upstream. Young Brazee gave her *go ahead;* she bucked as the engine stroke reversed and became sluggish. Brazee cursed as he gripped the spokes. She moved, and he gave her the *full speed* bell.

To Haikes, it was all familiar routine. The *Queen* was ploughing downstream now, the Stars and Stripes whipping from her jackstaff. Haikes sat with one eye on

Brazee, glancing now to the wheel, now to the jackstaff
ball and the marks upon which it should be held. His eye
turned dour and hard. The river was on the rise.
Muddied, swirling water coursed swiftly. Driftwood,
snag-dead trunks sharply abristle, floated by caving
banks sodden with melted snows and spring rains. Snags
and deadheads — a chill in the words.

Ellet was pacing his quarterdeck. Suddenly he directed
an anxious shout at the pilot.

"Look out, there! Head her off — keep her out!"

With the words, the long bows of the *Queen* thumped,
her hull grated. Haikes sprang to his feet. The *Queen* was
in a cross current and headed straight for a mud bar, fully
covered but betrayed to any trained pilot's eye by a ripple
and a cluster of bobbing tree branches.

"Give me that wheel, quick!" he snapped. "You're off
your marks and worse!"

"She drags by the bows, blast it!" Brazee's twisted face
was beaded, the sinews fluted his bare arms as he
strained. "She's hell to steer! You can't manage her."

"I held that wheel day and night when you were in
didies," growled Haikes, and took the spokes. He felt her
out, steadied her, brought her on the mark, and damned
the snags. She fought him, yes. She was not herself; like a
hysterical woman, he thought, all out of balance and
trim. Still, she knew his touch, and the whiffs of the
rhythmic exhaust took on a friendly note.

"Better reduce speed," called the anxious Ellet. Haikes
laughed joyously.

"I'll thank you to observe the river practice. Don't give
orders to the pilot-house unless you want to make a
landing."

Strange talk to soldier ears, but this was river work.
The captain had his place, and so did the pilot; a captain
gave no say-so to the wheel. The pilot was the boss of the
house, and when the boat was in motion, he ran her. If he
wrecked her — then God help him, for no one else would!

The *Monarch* was churning along; a good man at her

wheel, whoever he was. In a long clear stretch, Haikes turned the wheel over to Brazee, who admired his work volubly. Thus swapping tricks, hour to hour, with a few snatches of sleep during the night, they made Cairo by the next noon. And there, Owen Haikes realized, he must have a reckoning with whoever was handling the *Monarch*. Of his own standing aboard here, there was no further doubt at all. Bigger things pended.

News ran riot through the boat, while both craft lay up for refueling. The Federal gunboats were two hundred miles downstream, off Point Craighead of the Arkansas shore; five of them, armor-plated but unable to pass Fort Pillow and the deadly packet-rams. Here were urgent orders to come on with the Ohio River rams. General Grant had opened the Tennessee river for transports; the Confederates were falling back. The rams were needed at once to help clear the river.

Colonel Ellet fidgeted while the wood came aboard. Haikes, however, stepped ashore and strode to the *Monarch,* and aboard her. He had to find out. He could see the pilot, brown of shaggy beard, leaning from the house and puffing at his pipe. Then he recognized the face. Roberts, Bill Roberts, once his partner on the *Queen*. As he strode up, Roberts gave him a nod and a steady look.

"I thought it was you, by the way you handled the *Queen*. More tricky than ever, eh? She must be a job to hold."

"Might be worse," said Haikes.

"I heard about the *General Scott,*" said Roberts. "Bad business. They floated her again, but you stayed sunk. I lost track of you. You're on the river now?"

"To serve in a pinch, here."

"Blast it, old man, I don't see how it happened with the *Scott!*" The voice of Roberts, friendly and wise, was warming to the heart. "Moonlit night, clear course, you on watch at the wheel. And by the testimony you stove her on an old hulk, when you had plenty of water either side the bar."

Haikes nodded. "I was in the house, but I didn't wreck the *Scott*. Jack Hughes, the second pilot, swore I did it and that I was drunk. Why? He wanted my berth. He had come on duty a trifle early, and I had turned the wheel over to him, stopping for a chat. The Federal board at St. Louis wouldn't believe me; I was jobbed, my papers canceled, and I couldn't get a hearing at Washington. My appeal's still there, pigeonholed. Yes, the *Scott* struck, all right. I can feel it yet. I dream about it sometimes."

"It's a hell of a thing to remember," said Roberts. "How'll you feel when another craft comes stem on to rip the guts out of you?"

"Probably won't be pleasant." Haikes gave him a look. "Why are you here?"

Roberts pointed with his pipe toward the flag on the jackstaff, mutely.

"I shipped under the name of Smith," said Haikes. The other grinned.

"Suits me, old man. Say, I hear George Montgomery commands the rams below."

Haikes nodded. "George is a good man, a master pilot; he was on the board of inquiry, and the only one who believed me. A Southerner, but good. Still," he added, ironically thinking of that letter from Montgomery, "I guess there's one or two things about a pilot he doesn't savvy."

"Yeah?" drawled Roberts. "I hear Jackson Hughes is down there, too. What'll you do if we run up ag'in him?"

Haikes flushed. "Ram him, damn him!"

"Shake!"

Roberts put out a hand. Haikes met the hard grip with his own; they exchanged one nod of comprehension, and parted.

Wood was aboard, and coal, and a couple of barrels of resin to rush up the steam gauge if need came. Haikes had the *Queen* now; she was his to handle. He heartened to the quick wave of the hand from Roberts, to the faint

105

jingle of the bell, the swift response of the threshing paddles.

The broad Mississippi was less cumbered with craft than the Ohio. The shore marks stirred his pilot's memories, the spokes of the tugging wheel grew warm to his clasp, the jack staff swung to his bidding. And Montgomery stood ready to let the *Queen* through to a traitorous job, eh? So much the worse for Montgomery.

River marks had changed, but the pilot's trained eye meant more than all else, and this changed not. It was a long watch, with some help from the mate, to the rendezvous off the Arkansas shore, above and opposite Fort Pillow.

The fleet of gunboats built at St. Louis were in waiting, huddled along the shore, squat and black, peaked shed roofs plated with railroad iron. Propeller craft, heavily gunned, but unwieldy, slow in turning.

Here was live news. The Confederate craft had steamed for Memphis; Fort Pillow was cut off and would be evacuated any day now. The *Lancaster* and the *Switzerland* came churning in. The towboat rams were somewhere behind with the coal barges.

Haikes, puffing at his pipe, heard Colonel Ellet's shrill exchange with the gunboat commander alongside.

"I have an independent command. I'll not stay here to be attacked at moorings! My boats are wooden rams, without a defensive gun. By Jupiter, I'll run the fort batteries and get to close quarters with those boats below!"

"You don't know those Rebel rams. They come on in spite of hell," was the reply. "I can't risk these gunboats until your whole fleet is here."

"I know my own boats, sir, and my own men. I'll match steamboat with steamboat. The rebels aren't the only ones in the ramming business!"

In the June night, gunboats and rams dropped down the river. The transports evacuating Fort Pillow had disappeared around a bend; the deserted fort was silent, dark. Forty miles to Memphis and the enemy fleet!

A dark night and misty. The column crept on at half speed, with lights shrouded.

The gunboat commander seemed to think that the enemy could be surprised at moorings, but Haikes laughed grimly at such nonsense. Not with George Montgomery on watch! A pilot who could not see his river in the night, reading the hushed sounds of current and shoreline, was no pilot. Surprise Montgomery? Not a chance.

The pilot-house was high and lonely. Haikes gloried in pitting himself against the current and the cranky *Queen;* she was inclined to jaw like a toad in a hailstorm, but he coaxed her, mastered her.

Roberts was having his own troubles with the *Monarch*. For tonight and tomorrow the old *Queen* was his, he reflected, and for the last time. Ram or be rammed, ram and be rammed, wreck her, sink her — crash!

Near midnight they tied up to the anchored gunboats, two miles short of Memphis.

Half past four, and dawn. The sky was brightening, but a white fog lay thick and damp upon the yellow river, veiling the Arkansas shore, dimming the bluff line of the Tennessee shore. The order came to cast off.

Haikes sent the *Queen* ahead on a slow bell. From the pilot-house, he could see the low shapes of gunboats in line for port and starboard, could see the spectral shape of the *Monarch* on his starboard beam, the *Lancaster* and *Switzerland* well astern.

The flag on the jack staff drooped with the mist; forward of the tall smoking stacks, between the bell and the jack. Colonel Ellet stood erect, a gamecock alert for battle. He held sword in one hand, speaking trumpet in the other. A fool place! The first shock from bows on would pitch him overboard.

The *Queen* yawed, as an eddy clutched her unwieldy prow. The colonel faced about.

107

"Straight down the river!" he barked. "Straight, I say!" "I'm at this wheel," rasped Haikes, all on edge. "You mind your business and I'll mind mine!"

The fog on the river began to settle, disclosing the curve of the Tennessee shore; there grew the Chickasaw Bluffs of Memphis, sprinkled with gables and spires and roof-tops, all sharpened by the sunrise glow.

Five o'clock. The sun was flooding the blue. The fog went rolling in ragged billows before the morning breeze, and here they came sallying out of Memphis — the Confederate craft, not waiting at bay but forging forth to the attack. The upper works of river packets swam upon the fog, moving islands overhung by volcanic plumes of black smoke. The low gunboats were dimmed shapes rifting the swirl of mist.

Haikes caught, to starboard and port, the piping of bosuns' whistles from the Union gunboats, the voices of officers. From his own boat the excited accents of the infantry lieutenant came rocketing up to the pilot-house, steadying the sharpshooters behind the forecastle bulkhead and along the bulwarks.

He glanced about. The gunboats were a bit behind. The sidewheel *Lancaster* and the sternwheel *Switzerland* were a third of a mile astern, wallowing as though in trouble. At the forefront were only the *Queen* and the *Monarch;* the latter was slightly out of line, off his starboard quarter.

One hand and a foot guarding the spokes of the big wheel, he seized the spyglass from its hooks and trained it. To his eye sprang the upper works of the steamboats surging through the thinned mist; the names on the panels beneath the house ledges jutted as though embossed.

On the right of the line was the *Beauregard* — a sidewheeler, by the upcurving wheel boxes. She was a big packet, unknown to him, probably renamed for this work. Another side-wheeler sprang into sight — the *General Price*. Haikes frowned as the mist blotted her briefly;

his glass swept on. The steamboats *Jeff Thompson, General Lovel*, and others, with gunboats; two lines breasting in, determined, bulking more largely as they shortened the distance to the channel.

He leveled again on the *Price* and *Beauregard*. An interval was between them, a wide and promising interval. He laughed harshly. Montgomery was making it easy for him, eh? No doubt, Montgomery knew by spies who were aboard here — knew more than the colonel in command! Take the *Queen* through, apparently miss his mark, and hand her over, eh? Damn Montgomery! Little he knew of the pride of a pilot!

He returned his gaze to the *Price*, frowning and puzzled. A quick, stabbing breath escaped him. By heavens, the old *General Scott!* The very ship he had been broken for piling up! The crown of her stacks, the large Anchor Line emblem still hanging between those high iron cylinders, the fancy work of her house, the gilt 'S' of the weather-vane atop her jack, where the Confederate flag fluttered out — the old *Scott* herself, rebuilt and renamed, but the same!

He focused upon the pilot-house, to pick out the figure at the helm. Suddenly he dropped the glass and braced to his own wheel, as smoke gushed from a gunboat. A thunderclap jarred the air and a shell whined over the fleet. Colonel Ellet, on the hurricane deck forward, lowered his glass, pivoted, and flourished his sword.

"Full speed ahead!" shrilled his voice. "Take the *Beauregard*, ram her. *Monarch* ahoy! Alf!" This to his brother. "Straight ahead and take the *Price!*"

The bellow of cannon shut off his words. Haikes yanked the full-speed bell. The escape pipes belched, the *Queen* trembled to the paddle-thresh, gathered new way. Cinders from the blackly streaming stacks volleyed against the pilot-house. Haikes drove her into the veiling powder smoke. He held the ball of her jack, with the flag flattened out by the breeze, upon the interval between the two opposing packets.

109

She fought him. Frightened, was she? Dreaded the crash, had no stomach for it; a ship knows, sometimes. He held her to it grimly. Brave men, down there in the engine-room, trusting to him. The infantry sharpshooters — poor devils, waiting for the bows to be stove and the timbers to splinter, tearing flesh from bones! Ellet was facing forward, tense, unfearing, gripping his foolish sword.

The smoke rolled aside. Here they came, parting smoke and water with their rush; *Beauregard* to left, the *Price* to right, clearly revealed. Bulwarked with cotton bales, a brass field piece in the bows of each craft, paddle wheels churning, stems and sides in a slather of spray, pilots aloft bent to the spokes and peering through the windows. That interval — they were leaving it for him! Once he was well into it, both boats would converge on the *Monarch* and smash her.

All in a moment, now. Time was short, space lessened. The racing *Queen* bore on with the current swifter than the pair heading upstream could cleave it. Haikes gripped the *Price* with his gaze. Yes, she was the old *Scott,* for sure. No need of a glass now. Pilot house and pilot's bearded shaggy face under the visored cap shot forward into view like a picture in a stereoscope.

Hughes — Jack Hughes — there at the wheel of the *Price!*

The *Beauregard* was leading her consort. The *Queen,* in a trembling shudder of power, was ahead of the *Monarch.* From the corner of his eye, Haikes discerned the speed of each craft, the intersection of invisible lines; as he gripped the spokes, he knew by instinct what must happen, what could not be avoided. The wheel spun, all his weight suddenly upon it.

Suddenly and swiftly, disregarding the frantic yelp from Ellet, the *Queen* swerved away from the *Beauregard,* cut across the bows of the *Monarch.* Haikes jerked the bell for more speed. His jackstaff ball held for the jack of the *Price,* lined it like a rifle sight, so that the staff cut the face of Hughes at the wheel ahead.

"Ram him, damn him!" The yell burst from Haikes. "You, Hughes, Jack Hughes! Come on, blast you, come on!"

Guns were thundering, carbines and rifles banging away. Hughes must have seen the lean, blazing-eyed face heading for him. Was he game to hold on, take it bows for bows and crash to hell? A hundred yards, seventy-five, fifty — by the Eternal! The *Price* fell off, veered. Hughes, with guilt on his soul —

Twenty yards. A picture of Hughes with an astonished squint, mouth agape, hands twirling the spokes desperately, and in vain! The *Queen*'s jackstaff blotted out the 'P' of the "Price" on the paddle-wheel box. A wild, harsh laugh burst from Haikes. Ram him, damn him — no escape now!

Then in, with a heave and a crash that echoed from shore to shore.

Plastered against the wheel by the shock, Haikes missed nothing. The stacks wavered but held. Ellet was down on his knees. Men were shouting, but the nose of the *Queen* was buried deep into the splintered wheelbox of the *Price*. The *Price* was heaved up, careening. Her stacks came down with another terrific crash. Hughes barely escaped as he scrambled clear of the pilot-house.

Haikes gave the backing bell. The *Queen* was wedged, hanging like a bulldog, dragging the *Price* with her as she backed. They swung in an arc — then she tore free.

All was smoke and bedlam. Surprised by the sudden move of Haikes, but obeying the orders given him, Bill Roberts had brought the *Monarch* straight on.

The *Beauregard,* over-reaching, had whirled with one engine reversed and wheel hard down; at full speed again, she was lining for the *Monarch*. She was fast, too fast! She would get the *Monarch* broadside before Roberts could head about and straighten out.

No, by God! Back the *Queen* and keep a-backing — stave her in, wreck her! The old girl would prefer it, and would die with honors. She was between the *Beauregard* and the *Monarch* now. Haikes heard bullets whistling and pelting around him as he gripped the spokes for that final spin and twirl.

The *Beauregard* roared in on vengeance bent, bow gun vomiting a shell, rifles spitting and crackling. The shell landed — wham! Ellet was down, with a bullet through one leg. The *Queen,* her bow buckled awry, slewed from her rudders; Haikes, with a yell, leaned on his wheel with every ounce of strength. The *Beauregard* loomed to port, shutting out the sky. The gaunt face of her pilot grinned over the wheel-spokes as he spat out his cigar and braced himself for the shock. God help the maindeck crews!

The *Beauregard,* with iron-plated ram jutting, struck. The old *Queen* took it, but not with her full broadside. Haikes, with his last work at the huge wheel, evaded that. She reeled as beak and bow ripped and ground along her guards, crushing wheel box and hull and flinging her to starboard. The *Beauregard* sheared on, reeling.

The *Queen* swung back to level. Haikes picked himself up, yelled defiantly, and jerked the bell to stop the engines; the one wheel remaining was thrashing wildly. The *Beauregard* had forged into the clear, trying frantically to change course. Too late! Roberts had swung the *Monarch.* He was boiling in to ram; he was not to be dodged. By the Lord — he was into her! He caught her just forward of her wheel housing, full slap!

Haikes shifted gaze to the *Price.* She was low in the water, going under. Who was at the wheel of the *Scott* this time, Jack Hughes? Claw off from that barge if you can!

The *Beauregard* was sinking from her bows, figures leaping over, Roberts backing away and clear of her. The *Queen,* drifting in the current, was wafted about while gunfire billowed. Only a bloody spot indicated the post of Ellet, up forward. Haikes looked at the Monarch. A wild, instinctive yell burst from him.

"Bill! Look out!"

The *Monarch* was backing in a circle, clear of the *Beauregard;* but the *Lovell* and the *Jeff Thompson* were racing for her, on port and starboard, to nip her between them — racing straight for her from either side!

Roberts was jerking the bell-cord. Stop — go ahead — full speed ahead! The paddle-wheels of the *Monarch* churned the water to froth. The *Monarch* almost reared up as she fought for way. She moved, took speed, moved faster and faster. Could she do it? She did, by a hair. A wild yell and another burst from Haikes as he saw her clear of that narrowing gap. The *Lovell* grazed her very stern. Then, bows on, the *Lovell* and the *Thompson* rammed each other.

A gunboat shell burst in the bowels of the *Lovell*. Her boiler let go with a tremendous concussion.

The Memphis levee was dense with watching thousands; the rooftops were serried with spectators. At last the tardy *Lancaster* and the *Switzerland* were pulling in, but the enemy signaled quits. A white flag blew on the *Lovell*. The *Thompson* was creeping for shore. The *Price* and *Beauregard* showed only a trace of stacks or upper works. Crippled gunboats and rams made for safety.

Haikes rang the engine-room. The men were still on duty. With her one wheel at slow speed and her rudders hard over, the *Queen* fluttered like a winged duck for the nearest shoals. She was listing heavily.

With a final creak of shattered timbers, with a groan and a lurch, the old *Queen* heaved herself aground and halted. The *Monarch* came wobbling in with crooked beak, and hung poised. Haikes was thinking now of Washington, of his appeal pigeonholed there, of what all this day's work might mean in his future. Then he found Bill Roberts hailing him from the other pilot-house, hanging out, grinning at him.

"Hey, there! Need any help?"

"Hell, no!" rejoined Haikes joyously. Roberts grinned again.

"Tit for tat, ram for ram! You missed orders, durn you! I was to take the *Price!*"

"Orders be hanged!" responded Haikes. "You saw what pilot she had, didn't you?"

Roberts uttered a delighted yelp. "You bet. Ram him, damn him — and you done it. Hurray!"

He waved his hand and the *Monarch* sheered off. Haikes grunted.

"Guess I'd better go tell Colonel Ellet the truth, huh? Ram him, damn him! Makes a pretty good motto . . ."

Fishhead

IRVIN S. COBB

It goes past the powers of my pen to try to describe Reelfoot Lake for you so that you, reading this, will get the picture of it in your mind as I have it in mind.

For Reelfoot Lake is like no other lake that I know anything about. It is an afterthought of Creation.

The rest of this continent was made and had dried in the sun for thousands of years — millions of years, for all I know — before Reelfoot came to be. It's the newest big thing in nature on this hemisphere, probably, for it was formed by the great earthquake of 1811.

That earthquake of 1811 surely altered the face of the earth on the then far frontier of this country.

It changed the course of rivers, it converted hills into what are now the sunk lands of three states, and it turned the solid ground to jelly and made it roll in waves like the sea.

And in the midst of the retching of the land and the vomiting of the waters it depressed to varying depths a

section of the earth crust sixty miles long, taking it down
— trees, hills, hollows, and all; and a crack broke through
to the Mississippi River so that for three days the river
ran up stream, filling the hole.

The result was the largest lake south of the Ohio, lying
mostly in Tennessee, but extending up across what is
now the Kentucky line, and taking its name from a fancied resemblance in its outline to the splay, reeled foot of
a cornfield negro. Nigger-wool Swamp, not so far away,
may have got its name from the same man who
christened Reelfoot; at least so it sounds.

Reelfoot is, and has always been, a lake of mystery.

In places it is all but bottomless. Other places the
skeletons of the cypress-trees that went down when the
earth sank, still stand upright so that if the sun shines
from the right quarter, and the water is less muddy than
common, a man, peering face downward into its depths,
sees, or thinks he sees, down below him the bare top-
limbs upstretching like drowned men's fingers, all coated
with the mud of years and bandaged with pennons of the
green lake slime.

In still other places the lake is shallow for long
stretches, no deeper than breast high to a man, but dangerous because of the weed growths and the sunken
drifts which entangle a swimmer's limbs. Its banks are
mainly mud, its waters are muddied, too, being a rich
coffee color in the spring and a copperish yellow in the
summer, and the trees along its shore are mud-colored
clear up their lower limbs after the spring floods, when
the dried sediment covers their trunks with a thick,
scrofulous-looking coat.

There are stretches of unbroken woodland around it,
and slashes where the cypress knees rise countlessly like
headstones for the dead snags that rot in the soft ooze.

There are dead-endings with the lowland corn growing
high and rank below and the bleached, fire-girdled trees
rising above, barren of leaf and limb.

There are long, dismal floats where in the spring the

clotted frog-spawn cling like patches of white mucus among the weed-stalks, and at night the turtles crawl out to lay clutches of perfectly round, white eggs with tough, rubbery shells in the sand. There are bayous leading off to nowhere, and sloughs that wind aimlessly, like great, blind worms, to finally join the big river that rolls a few miles to the westward.

So Reelfoot lies there, flat in the bottoms, freezing lightly in the winter, steaming torridly in the summer, swollen in the spring when the woods have turned a vivid green and the buffalo-gnats by the million and the billion fill the flooded hollows with their pestilential buzzing, and in the fall, ringed about gloriously with all the colors which the first frost brings — gold of hickory, yellow-russet of sycamore, red of dogwood and ash, and purple-black of sweet-gum.

But the Reelfoot country has its uses. It is the best game and fish country, natural or artificial, that is left in the South today.

In their appointed seasons the duck and the geese flock in, and even semi-tropical birds, like the brown pelican and the Florida snake-bird, have been known to come there to nest.

Pigs, gone back to wildness, range the ridges, each razor-backed drove captained by a gaunt, savage, slab-sided old boar. By night the bullfrogs, inconceivably big and tremendously vocal, bellow under the banks.

It is a wonderful place for fish — bass and crappies, and perch, and the snouted buffalo fish.

How these edible sorts live to spawn, and how their spawn in turn live to spawn again is a marvel, seeing how many of the big fish-eating cannibal-fish there are in Reelfoot.

Here, bigger than anywhere else, you find the garfish, all bones and appetite and horny plates, with a snout like an alligator, the nearest link, naturalists say, between the animal life of today and the animal life of the Reptilian Period.

The shovel-nose cat, really a deformed kind of freshwater sturgeon, with a great fan-shaped membranous plate jutting out from his nose like a bowsprit, jumps all day in the quiet places with mighty splashing sounds, as though a horse had fallen into the water.

On every stranded log the huge snapping turtles lie on sunny days in groups of four and six, baking their shells black in the sun, with their little snaky heads raised watchfully, ready to slip noiselessly off at the first sound of oars grating in the row-locks. But the biggest of them all are the catfish!

These are monstrous creatures, these catfish of Reelfoot — scaleless, slick things, with corpsy, dead eyes and poisonous fins, like javelins, and huge whiskers dangling from the sides of their cavernous heads.

Six and seven feet long they grow to be, and weigh 200 pounds or more, and they have mouths wide enough to take in a man's foot or a man's fist, and strong enough to break any hook save the strongest, and greedy enough to eat anything, living or dead or putrid, that the horny jaws can master.

Oh, but they are wicked things, and they tell wicked tales of them down there. They call them man-eaters, and compare then, in certain of their habits, to sharks.

Fishhead was of a piece with this setting.

He fitted into it as an acorn fits its cup. All his life he had lived on Reelfoot, always in the one place, at the mouth of a certain slough.

He had been born there, of a Negro father and a half-breed Indian mother, both of them now dead, and the story was that before his birth his mother was frightened by one of the big fish, so that the child came into the world most hideously marked.

Anyhow, Fishhead was a human monstrosity, the veritable embodiment of nightmare!

He had the body of a man — a short-stocky, sinewy

body — but his face was as near to being the face of a great fish as any face could be and yet retain some trace of human aspect.

His skull sloped back so abruptly that he could hardly be said to have a forehead at all; his chin slanted off right into nothing. His eyes were small and round with shallow, glazed, pale-yellow pupils, and they were set wide apart in his head, and they were unwinking and staring, like a fish's eyes.

His nose was no more than a pair of tiny slits in the middle of the yellow mask. His mouth was the worst of all. It was the awful mouth of a catfish, lipless and almost inconceivably wide, stretching from side to side.

Also when Fishhead became a man grown his likeness to a fish increased, for the hair upon his face grew out into two tightly kinked slender pendants that drooped down either side of the mouth like the beards of a fish!

If he had any other name than Fishhead, none excepting he knew it. As Fishhead he was known, and as Fishhead he answered. Because he knew the waters and the woods of Reelfoot better than any other man there, he was valued as a guide by the city men who came every year to hunt or fish; but there were few such jobs that Fishhead would take.

Mainly he kept to himself, tending his corn-patch, netting the lake, trapping a little, and in season pot hunting for the city markets. His neighbors, ague-bitten whites and malaria-proof Negroes alike, left him to himself.

Indeed, for the most part they had a superstitious fear of him. So he lived alone, with no kith nor kin, nor even a friend, shunning his kind and shunned by them.

His cabin stood just below the State line, where Mud Slough runs into the lake. It was a shack of logs, the only human habitation for four miles up or down.

Behind it the thick timber came shouldering right up to the edge of Fishhead's small truck patch, enclosing it in thick shade except when the sun stood just overhead.

He cooked his food in a primitive fashion, outdoors,

over a hole in the soggy earth or upon the rusted red ruin of an old cookstove, and he drank the saffron water of the lake out of a dipper made of a gourd, faring and fending for himself, a master hand at skiff and net, competent with duck-gun and fishspear, yet a creature of affliction and loneliness, part savage, almost amphibious, set apart from his fellows, silent and suspicious.

In front of his cabin jutted out a long fallen cottonwood trunk, lying half in and half out of the water, its top side burnt by the sun and worn by the friction of Fishhead's bare feet until it showed countless patterns of tiny scrolled lines, its underside black and rotted, and lapped at unceasingly by little waves like tiny licking tongues.

Its farther end reached deep water. And it was a part of Fishhead, for no matter how far his fishing and trapping might take him in the daytime, sunset would find him back there, his boat drawn up on the bank, and he on the other end of this log.

From a distance men had seen him there many times, sometimes squatted motionless as the big turtles that would crawl upon its dipping tip in his absence, sometimes erect and motionless like a creek crane, his misshapen yellow form outlined against the yellow sun, the yellow water, the yellow banks — all of them yellow together.

If the Reelfooters shunned Fishhead by day they feared him by night and avoided him as a plague, dreading even the chance of a casual meeting. For there were ugly stories about Fishhead — stories which all the Negroes and some of the whites believed.

They said that a cry which had been heard just before dusk and just after, skittering across the darkened waters, was his calling cry to the big catfish, and at his bidding they came trooping in, and that in their company he swam in the lake on moonlight nights, sporting with them, diving with them, even feeding with them on what manner of unclean things.

The cry had been heard many times, that much was

certain, and it was certain also that the big fish were noticeably thick at the mouth of Fishhead's slough. No native Reelfooter, white or black, would willingly wet a leg or an arm there.

Here Fishhead had lived, and here he was going to die. The Baxters were going to kill him, and this day in late summer was to be the time of the killing.

The two Baxters — Jake and Joel — were coming in their dugout to do it!

This murder had been a long time in the making. The Baxters had to brew their hate over a slow fire for months before it reached the pitch of action.

They were poor whites, poor in everything, repute, and world goods, and standing — a pair of fever-ridden squatters who lived on whiskey and tobacco when they could get it, and on fish and cornbread when they couldn't.

The feud itself was of months' standing.

Meeting Fishhead one day in the spring on the spindly scaffolding of the skiff landing at Walnut Log, and being themselves far overtaken in liquor and vainglorious with a bogus alcoholic substitute for courage, the brothers had accused him, wantonly and without proof, of running their trot-line and stripping it of the hooked catch — an unforgivable sin among the water dwellers and the shanty boaters of the South.

Seeing that he bore this accusation in silence, only eyeing them steadfastly, they had been emboldened then to slap his face, whereupon he turned and gave them both the beating of their lives — bloodying their noses and bruising their lips with hard blows against their front teeth, and finally leaving them, mauled and prone, in the dirt.

Moreover, in the onlookers a sense of the everlasting fitness of things had triumphed over race prejudice and allowed them — two freeborn, sovereign whites — to be licked by a nigger! Therefore they were going to get the nigger!

The whole thing had been planned out amply. They

were going to kill him on his log at sundown. There would be no witnesses to see it, no retribution to follow after it. The very ease of the undertaking made them forget even their inborn fear of the place of Fishhead's habitation.

For more than an hour they had been coming from their shack across a deeply indented arm of the lake. Their dugout, fashioned by fire and adz and draw-knife from the bole of a gum-tree, moved through the water as noiselessly as a swimming mallard, leaving behind it a long, wavy trail on the stilled waters.

Jake, the better oarsman, sat flat in the stern of the round bottomed craft, paddling with quick, splashless strokes. Joel, the better shot, was squatted forward. There was a heavy, rusted duckgun between his knees.

Though their spying upon the victim had made them certain sure he would not be about the shore for hours, a doubled sense of caution led them to hug closely the weedy banks. They slid along the shore like shadows, moving so swiftly and in such silence that the watchful mud turtles barely turned their snaky heads as they passed.

So, a full hour before the time, they came slipping around the mouth of the slough and made for a natural ambuscade which the mixed-breed had left within a stone's jerk of his cabin to his own undoing.

Where the slough's flow joined deeper water a partly uprooted tree was stretched, prone from shore, at the top still thick and green with leaves that drew nourishment from the earth in which the half uncovered roots yet held, and twined about with an exuberance of trumpet vines and wild fox-grapes. All about was a huddle of drift — last year's cornstalks, shreddy strips of bark, chunks of rotted weed, all the riffle and dunnage of a quiet eddy.

Straight into this green clump glided the dugout and swung, broadside on, against the protecting trunk of the tree, hidden from the inner side by the intervening curtains of rank growth, just as the Baxters had intended it should be hidden, when days before in their scouting they marked this masked place of waiting and included it, then and there, in the scope of their plans.

There had been no hitch or mishap. No one had been abroad in the late afternoon to mark their movements — and in a little while Fishhead ought to be due. Jake's woodman's eyes followed the downward swing of the sun speculatively.

The shadows, thrown shoreward, lengthened and slithered on the small ripples. The small noises of the day died out; the small noises of the coming night began to multiply.

The green bodied flies went away and big mosquitoes, with speckled gray legs, came to take the place of the flies.

The sleepy lake sucked at the mud banks with small mouthing sounds, as though it found the taste of the raw mud agreeable. A monster crawfish, big as a chicken lobster, crawled out of the top of his dried mud chimney and perched himself there, an armored sentinel on the watchtower.

Bull bats began to flitter back and forth, above the tops of the trees. A pudgy muskrat, swimming with head up, was moved to sidle off briskly as he met a cotton-mouth moccasin snake, so fat and swollen with summer poison that it looked almost like a legless lizard as it moved along the surface of the water in a series of slow torpid 's's. Directly above the head of either of the waiting assassins a compact little swarm of midges hung, holding to a sort of kite-shaped formation.

A little more time passed and Fishhead came out of the woods at the back, walking swiftly, with a sack over his shoulder.

For a few seconds his deformities showed in the clearing, then the black inside of the cabin swallowed him up.

By now the sun was almost down. Only the red hub of it showed above the timber line across the lake, and the shadows lay inland a long way. Out beyond, the big cats were stirring, and the great smacking sounds as their twisting bodies leaped clear and fell back in the water, came shoreward in a chorus.

But the two brothers, in their green covert, gave heed to nothing except the one thing upon which their hearts were set and their nerves tensed. Joel gently shoved his gun-barrels across the log, cuddling the stock to his shoulder and slipping two fingers caressingly back and forth upon the triggers. Jake held the narrow dugout steady by a grip upon a fox-grape tendril.

A little wait and then the finish came!

Fishhead emerged from the cabin door and came down the footpath to the water and out upon the water on his log.

He was barefooted and bareheaded, his cotton shirt open down the front to show his yellow neck and breast, his dungaree trousers held about his waist by a twisted tow string.

His broad splay feet, with the prehensile toes outspread, gripped the polished curve of the log as he moved along its swaying, dipping surface, until he came to its outer end, and stood there erect, his chest filling, his chinless face lifted up, and something of mastership and determination in his poise.

And then — his eye caught what another's eyes might have missed — the round, twin ends of the gun barrels, the fixed gleam of Joel's eyes, aimed at him through the green tracery!

In that swift passage of time, too swift almost to be measured by seconds, realization flashed all through him, and he threw his head still higher and opened wide his shapeless trap of a mouth, and out across the lake he sent skittering and rolling his cry.

And in his cry was the laugh of a loon, and the croaking bellow of a frog, and the bay of a hound, all the compounded night noises of the lake. And in it, too, was a farewell, and a defiance, and an appeal!

The heavy roar of the duck gun came!

124

At twenty yards the double charge tore the throat out of him. He came down, face forward, upon the log and clung there, his trunk twisting distortedly, his legs twitching and kicking like the legs of a speared frog; his shoulders hunching and lifting spasmodically as the life ran out of him all in one swift coursing flow.

His head canted up between the heaving shoulders, his eyes looked full on the staring face of his murderer, and then the blood came out of his mouth, and Fishhead, in death still as much fish as man, slid, flopping, head first, off the end of the log, and sank, face downward slowly, his limbs all extended.

One after another a string of big bubbles came up to burst in the middle of a widening reddish stain on the coffee-colored water.

The brothers watched this, held by the horror of the thing they had done, and the cranky dugout, having been tipped far over by the recoil of the gun, took water steadily across its gunwale; and now there was a sudden stroke from below upon its careening bottom and it went over and they were in the lake.

But shore was only twenty feet away, the trunk of the uprooted tree only five. Joel, still holding fast to his shot gun, made for the log, gaining it with one stroke. He threw his free arm over it and clung there, treading water, as he shook his eyes free.

Something gripped him — some great, sinewy, unseen thing gripped him fast by the thigh, crushing down on his flesh!

He uttered no cry, but his eyes popped out, and his mouth set in a square shape of agony, and his fingers gripped into the bark of the tree like grapples. He was pulled down and down, by steady jerks, not rapidly but steadily, so steadily, and as he went his fingernails tore four little white strips in the tree-bark. His mouth went under, next his popping eyes, then his erect hair, and finally his clawing, clutching hand, and that was the end of him.

Jake's fate was harder still, for he lived longer, long enough to see Joel's finish. He saw it through the water that ran down his face, and with a great surge of his whole body, he literally flung himself across the log and jerked his legs up high into the air to save them. He flung himself too far, though, for his face and chest hit the water on the far side.

And out of this water rose the head of a great fish, with the lake slime of years on its flat, black head, its whiskers bristling, its corpsy eyes alight. Its horny jaws closed and clamped in the front of Jake's shirt. His hand struck out wildly and was speared on a poisoned fin, and, unlike Joel, he went from sight with a great yell, and a whirling and churning of the water that made the cornstalks circle on the edges of a small whirlpool.

But the whirlpool soon thinned away into widening rings of ripples, and the cornstalks quit circling and became still again, and only the multiplying night noises sounded about the mouth of the slough.

The bodies of all three came ashore on the same day near the same place. Except for the gaping gunshot wound where the neck met the chest, Fishhead's body was unmarked.

But the bodies of the two Baxters were so marred and mauled that the Reelfooters buried them together on the bank without ever knowing which might be Jake's and which might be Joel's.

On the Lake

ELLEN DOUGLAS

Late summer in Philippi is a deadly time of year. Other parts of the United States are hot, it is true, but not like the lower Mississippi Valley. Here the shimmering heat — the thermometer standing day after day in the high nineties and the nights breathless and oppressive — is compounded, even in a drought, by the saturated air. Thunderheads, piling up miles high in the afternoon sky, dwarf the great jet planes that fly through them. The air is heavy with moisture, but for weeks in July and August there is no rain.

In July, Lake Okatukla begins to fall. The lake, named from a meandering bayou that flows into it on the Arkansas side, bounds the town of Philippi on the west. It was once a horseshoe-shaped bend of the Mississippi, but its northern arm is blocked off from the river now by the Nine-Mile Dike, built years ago when a cut-through was made to straighten the river's course. The southern arm of the lake is still a channel into the Mississippi, through which pass towboats pushing strings of barges loaded with gravel, sand, cotton, scrap iron, soybeans, fertilizer, or oil.

In August, the lake drops steadily lower, and at the foot of the levee mud flats begin to appear around the rusty barges that serve as Philippi's municipal terminal and around the old stern-wheeler moored just above them that has been converted into the Philippi Yacht Club. The surface of the mud, covered with discarded beer cans, broken bottles, and tangles of baling wire, cracks and scales like the skin of some scrofulous river beast, and a deathlike stench pervades the hot, still air. But the lake is deep and broad — more than a mile wide at the bend, close to the town — and fifty feet out from the lowest mud flat the steely surface water hides unplumbed black depths.

Late in August, if rain falls all along the course of the Mississippi, there will be a rise of the lake as the river backs into it. The mud flats are covered again. The trees put on pale spikes of new growth. The sandbars are washed clean. Mud runnels stream from the rain-heavy willow fronds, and the willows lift their heads. The fish begin to bite. For a week or two, from the crest of the rise, when the still water begins to clear, dropping the mud that the river has poured into the lake, until another drop has begun to expose the mud flats, Lake Okatukla is beautiful — a serene, broad wilderness of green trees and bright water, bounded at the horizon by the green range of levee sweeping in a slow curve against the sky. Looking down into the water, one can see through drifting forests of moss the quick flash of frightened bream, the shadowy threat of great saw-toothed gar. In the town, there has been little to do for weeks but wait out the heat. Only a few Negroes have braved the stench of the mud flats for the sake of a slimy catfish or a half-dead bream. After the rise, however, fishermen are out again in their skiffs, casting for bass around the trunks of the big willow trees or fishing with cane poles and minnows for white perch along the fringe willows. Family parties picnic here and there along the shore. The lake is big — twelve miles long, with dozens of curving inlets and white sandy islands. Hundreds of fishermen can spend their day trolling its shores and scarcely disturb one another.

One morning just after the August rise a few years ago, Anna Glover set out with two of her three sons, Ralph and Steve, and one of Ralph's friends, Murray McCrae, for a day on the lake. Her oldest son, who at fifteen considered himself too old for such family expeditions, and her husband, Richard, an architect, for whom summer was the busiest season of the year, had stayed behind. It was early, and the waterfront was deserted when Anna drove over the crest of the levee. She parked the car close to the Yacht Club mooring float, where the Glovers kept their fishing skiff tied up, and began to unload the gear — life jackets for the children, tackle box, bait, poles, gas can, and Skotch cooler full of beer, soft drinks, and sandwiches. She had hardly begun when she thought she heard someone shouting her name. "Miss Anna! Hey, Miss Anna!" She looked around, but, seeing the whole slope of the levee empty and no one on the deck of the Yacht Club except Gaines Williamson, the Negro bartender, she called the children back from the water's edge, toward which they had run as soon as the car stopped, and began to distribute the gear among them to carry down to the float.

Anna heaved the heavy cooler out of the car without much effort and untied the poles from the rack on the side of the car, talking as she worked. At thirty-six, she looked scarcely old enough to have three half-grown sons. Her high, round brow was unlined, her brown eyes were clear, and her strong, boyish figure in shorts and a tailored shirt looked almost like a child's. She wore her long sandy-brown hair drawn into a twist on the back of

129

her head. Ralph and his friend Murray were ten; Steve was seven. Ralph's straight nose, solemn expression, and erect, sway-backed carriage made him look like a small preacher. Steve was gentler, with brown eyes like his mother's, fringed by a breathtaking sweep of dark lashes. They were beautiful children, or so Anna thought, for she regarded them with the most intense, subjective passion. Murray was a slender, dark boy with a closed face and a reserve that to Anna seemed impregnable. They were picking up the gear to move it down to the Yacht Club float when they all heard someone calling, and turned around.

"Ralph! Hey there, boys! Here I am, up here!" the voice cried.

"It's Estella, Mama," Ralph said. "There she is, over by the barges."

"Hi, Estella!" Steve shouted. He and Ralph put down the poles and cooler and ran along the rough, uneven slope of the levee, jumping over the iron rings set in the concrete to hold the mooring lines and over the rusty cables that held the terminal barges against the levee.

"Come on, Murray," Anna said. "Let's go speak to Estella. She's over there fishing off the ramp."

Sitting on the galvanized-iron walkway from the levee to the terminal, her legs dangling over the side of the walkway ten feet above the oily surface of the water, was Estella Moseby, a huge and beautiful Negro woman who had worked for the Glover family since the children were small. She had left them a few months before to have a child and had stayed home afterward, at James's, her husband's, insistence, to raise her own family. It was the first time that Anna or the children had seen her since shortly after the child was born. Estella held a long cane pole in one hand and with the other waved toward Anna and the children. Her serene, round face was golden brown, the skin flawless even in the cruel light of the August sun, her black hair pulled severely back to a knot on her neck, her enormous dark eyes and wide mouth smiling with pleasure at the unexpected meeting. As the children approached, she drew her line out of the water and pulled herself up by the cable that served as a side rail for the walkway. The walk creaked under her shifting weight. She was fully five feet ten inches tall — at least seven inches taller than Anna — and loomed above the heads of the little group on the levee like an amiable golden giantess, her feet set wide apart to support the weight that fleshed her big frame. Her gaily flowered house dress, printed with daisies and morning-glories in shades of blue, green, and yellow, took on the very quality of her appearance, as if she were some tropical fertility goddess robed to receive her worshippers.

"Lord, Estella," Anne said. "Come on down. We haven't seen you in ages. How have you been?"

"You see me," Estella said. "Fat as ever." She carefully wrapped her line around her pole, secured the hook in the cork, and came down from her high perch to join the others on the levee. "Baby or no baby, I got to go fishing after such a fine rain," she said.

"We're going on a picnic," Steve said.

"Well, isn't that fine," Estella said. "Where is your brother?"

"Oh, he thinks he's too old to associate with us any more," Anna said. "He *scorns* us. How is the baby?"

The two women looked at each other with the shy pleasure of old friends long separated who have not yet fallen back into the easy ways of their friendship.

"Baby's fine," Estella said. "My cousin Bernice is nursing him. I said to myself this morning, 'I haven't been fishing since I got pregnant with Lee Roy. I *got* to go fishing.' So look at me. Here I am sitting on this ramp since seven this morning and no luck."

Steve threw his arms around her legs. "Estella, why don't you come *work* for us again?" he said. "We don't like *anybody* but you."

"I'm coming, honey," she said. "Let me get these kids up a little bit and I'll be back."

"Estella, why don't you go fishing with us today?"
Ralph said. "We're going up to the north end of the lake
and fish all day."

"Yes, come on," Anna said. "Come on and keep me company. You can't catch any fish around this old barge, and
if you do they taste like fuel oil. I heard the bream are
really biting in the upper lake — over on the other side,
you know, in the willows."

Estella hesitated, looking out over the calm and shining dark water. "I ain't much on boats," she said. "Boats
make me nervous."

"Oh, come on, Estella," Anna said. "You know you
want to go."

"Well, it's the truth, I'm not catching any fish sitting
here. I got two little no-'count bream on my stringer." Estella paused, and then she said, "*All* y'all going to fish
from the boat? I'll crowd you."

"We're going to find a good spot and fish off the bank,"
Anna said. "We're already too many to fish from the
boat."

"Well, it'll be a pleasure," Estella said. "I'll just come
along. Let me get my stuff." She went up on the walkway
again and gathered up her tackle where it lay — a brown
paper sack holding sinkers, floats, hooks, and line, and
her pole and a coffee can full of worms and dirt.

"I brought my gig along," Ralph said as they all
trudged across the levee toward the Yacht Club. "I'm going to gig one of those great big buffalo or a gar or
something."

"Well, if you do, give it to me, honey," Estella said.
"James is really crazy about buffalo the way I cook it."
Pulling a coin purse out of her pocket, she turned to
Anna. "You reckon you might get us some beer in the
Yacht Club? A nice can of beer 'long about eleven o'clock
would be good."

"I've got two cans in the cooler," Anna said, "but maybe
we'd better get a couple more." She took the money and,
while Murray and Ralph brought the skiff around from

the far side of the Yacht Club, where it was tied up, went into the bar and bought two more cans of beer. Estella and Steve, meanwhile, carried the fishing gear down to the float.

Gaines Williamson, a short, powerfully built man in his forties, followed Anna out of the bar and helped stow their gear in the little boat. The children got in first and then helped Estella in. "Lord, Miss Estella," he said, "you too big for this boat, and that's a fact." He stood back and looked down at her doubtfully, sweat shining on his face and standing in droplets on his shaven scalp.

"I must say it's none of your business," Estella said.

"We'll be all right, Gaines," Anna said. "The lake's smooth as glass."

The boys held the skiff against the float while Anna got in, and they set out, cruising slowly up the lake until they found a spot that Estella and Anna agreed looked promising. Here, on a long, clean sandbar fringed with willows, they beached the boat. The children stripped off their life jackets, pulled off the jeans they wore over their swimming trunks, and began to wade.

"You children wade here in the open water," Estella ordered. "Don't go over yonder on the other side of the bar, where the willows are growing. You'll bother the fish."

She and Anna stood looking around. Wilderness was all about them. As far as they could see on either side of the lake, not even a road ran down to the water's edge. While they watched, two white herons dragged themselves awkwardly into the air and flapped away, long legs trailing. The southern side of the sandbar, where they had beached the boat, had no trees growing on it, but the edge of the northern side, which curved in on itself and out again, was covered with willows. Here the land was higher. Beyond a low hummock crowned with cottonwood trees, Anna and Estella discovered a pool, twenty-five yards long and nearly as wide, that had been left behind by the last rise, a few days before. Fringe willows grew all around it, and the fallen trunk of a huge cottonwood lay with its roots exposed on the ground, its whole length stretched out into the still water of the pool.

"Here's the place," Estella said decidedly. "Shade for us, and fringe willows for the fish. And looka there." She pointed to the fallen tree. "If there aren't any fish under *there* . . ." They stood looking down at the pool, pleased with their find.

"I'll go get our things," Estella said. "You sit down and rest yourself, Miss Anna."

"I'll come help you."

The two women unloaded the boat, and Anna carried the cooler up the low hill and left it in the shade of one of the cottonwood trees. Then they gathered the fishing tackle and took it over to a shady spot by the pool. In a few minutes, the children joined them, and Anna passed out poles and bait. The bream were rising to crickets, and she had brought a wire cylinder basket full of them.

"You boys scatter out, now," Anna said. "There's plenty of room for everybody, and if you stay too close together you'll hook each other."

Estella helped Steve bait his hook, then baited her own and dropped it into the water as close as she could get it to the trunk of the fallen tree. Almost as soon as it reached the water, her float began to bob and quiver.

"Here we go," she said in a low voice. "Take it under, now. Take it under." She addressed herself to the business of fishing with such delight and concentration that Anna stopped in the middle of rigging a pole to watch her. Even the children, intent on finding places for themselves, turned back to see Estella catch a fish. She stood over the pool like a priestess at her altar, all expectation and willingness, holding the pole lightly, as if her fingers could read the intentions of the fish vibrating through line and pole. Her bare arms were tense, and she gazed down into the still water. A puff of wind made the leafy shadows waver and tremble on the pool, and the float rocked deceptively. Estella's arms quivered with a jerk begun and suppressed. Her flowery dress flapped around her legs, and her skin shone with sweat and oil where the sunlight struck through the leaves across her forehead and down one cheek.

"Not yet," she muttered. "*Take* it." The float bobbed and went under. "Aaah!" She gave her line a quick, short jerk to set the hook; the line tightened, the long pole bent, and she swung a big bream out onto the sand. The fish flopped off the hook and down the slope toward the water; she dropped the pole and dived at it, half falling. Ralph, who had been watching, was ahead of her, shouting with excitement, grabbing up the fish before it could flop back into the pool, and putting it into Estella's hands, careful to avoid the sharp dorsal fin.

"Look, boys, look!" she cried happily. "Just look at him!" She held out the big bream, as wide and thick as her hand, marked with blue around the gills and orange on its swollen belly. The fish twisted and gasped in her hand while she got the stringer. She slid the metal end of the stringer through one gill and out the mouth, secured the other end to an exposed root of the fallen tree, and dropped the fish into the water, far enough away so that the bream's thrashing would not disturb their fishing spot.

"Quick now, Miss Anna," she said. "Get your line in there. I bet this pool is full of bream. Come on, boys, we're going to catch some fish today."

Anna baited her hook and dropped it in. The children scattered around the pool to their own places. In an hour, the two women had caught a dozen bream and four small catfish, and the boys had caught six or seven more bream. Then for ten minutes no one got a bite, and the boys began to lose interest. A school of minnows flashed into the shallow water at Anna's feet, and she pointed them out to Estella. "Bream are gone," she said. "They've quit feeding, or we wouldn't see any minnows."

Anna laid down her pole and told the children they could swim. "Come on, Estella," she said. "We can sit in the shade and watch them and have a beer, and then in a little while we can move to another spot."

"You aren't going to let them swim in this old lake, are you, Miss Anna?" Estella said.

"Sure. The bottom's nice and sandy here," Anna said. "Murray, your mama said you've got to keep your life preserver on if you swim." She said to Estella in a low voice, "He's not much of a swimmer. He's the only one I would worry about."

The children splashed and tumbled fearlessly in the water, Ralph and Steve popping up and disappearing, sometimes for so long that Anna, in spite of what she had said, would begin to watch anxiously for their blond heads.

"I must say, I don't see how you stand it," Estella said. "That water scares me."

"Nothing to be scared of," Anna said. "They're both good swimmers, and so am I. I could swim across the lake and back, I bet you, old as I am."

She fished two beers out of the Skotch cooler, opened them, and gave one to Estella. Then she sat down with her back against a cottonwood tree, gave Estella a cigarette, took one herself, and leaned back with a sigh. Estella sat down on a fallen log, and the two women smoked and drank their beer in silence for a few minutes. The breeze ran through the cottonwoods, shaking the leaves against each other. "I love the sound of the wind in a cottonwood tree," Anna said. "Especially at night when you wake up and hear it outside your window. I remember there was one outside the window of my room when I was a little girl, so close to the house I could climb out the window and get into it." The breeze freshened and the leaves pattered against each other. "It sounds cool," Anna said, "even in August."

"It's nice," Estella said. "Like a nice, light rain."

"Well, tell me what you've been doing with yourself,"

Anna said. "When are you going to move into your new house?"

"James wants to keep renting it out another year," Estella said. "He wants us to get ahead a little bit. And you know, Miss Anna, if I can hang on where I am we'll be in a good shape. We can rent that house until we finish paying for it, and then when we move we can rent the one we're in, and, you know, we own that little one next door, too. With four children now, we got to think of the future. And I must say, with all his old man's ways, James is a good provider. He looks after his own. So I go along with him. But, Lord, I can't stand it much longer. We're falling all over each other in that little tiny place. Kids under my feet all day. No place to keep the baby quiet. And in rainy weather! It's worse than a circus. I've gotten so all I do is yell at the kids. It would be a rest to go back to work."

"I wish you *would* come back to work," Anna said.

"No use talking about it," Estella said. "James says I've got to stay home at least until Lee Roy gets up to school age. And you can see for yourself I'd be paying out half what I made to get somebody to keep mine. But I'll tell you, my nerves are tore up."

"It takes a while to get your strength back after a baby," Anna said.

"Oh, I'm strong enough," Estella said. "It's not that." She pulled a stalk of Johnson grass and began to chew it thoughtfully. "I've had something on my mind," she said, "something I've been meaning to tell you ever since the baby came, and I haven't seen you by yourself — "

Anna interrupted her. "Look at the fish, Estella," she said. "They're really kicking up a fuss."

There was a wild, thrashing commotion in the water by the roots of the cottonwood tree where Estella had tied the stringer.

Estella watched a minute. "Lord, Miss Anna," she said, "something's after those fish. A turtle or something." She got up and started toward the pool as a long, dark, whip-like shape flung itself out of the water, slapped the

137

surface, and disappeared.

"Hey," Anna said, "it's a snake! A snake!"

Estella looked around for a weapon and hastily picked up a short, heavy stick and a rock from the ground. Moving lightly and easily in spite of her weight, she ran down to the edge of the water, calling over her shoulder, "I'll scare him off. I'll chunk him. Don't you worry." She threw the rock into the churning water, but it had no effect. "Go, snake. Leave our fish alone." She stood waving her stick threateningly over the water.

Anna came down to the pool now, and they both saw the whiplike form again. Fearlessly, Estella whacked at it with her stick.

"Keep back, Estella," Anna said. "He might bite you. Wait a minute and I'll get a longer stick."

"Go, snake!" Estella shouted furiously, confidently. "What's the matter with him? He won't go off. Go, you crazy snake!"

Now the children heard the excitement and came running across the beach and over the low hill where Estella and Anna had been sitting, to see what was happening.

"A snake, a snake!" Steve screamed. "He's after the fish. Come on, y'all! It's a big old snake after the fish."

The two older boys ran up. "Get 'em out of the water, Mama," Ralph said. "He's going to eat 'em."

"I'm scared he might bite me," Anna said. "Keep back. He'll go away in a minute." She struck at the water with the stick she had picked up.

Murray looked the situation over calmly. "Why don't we gig him?" he said to Ralph.

Ralph ran down to the boat and brought back the long, barb-pointed gig. "Move, Estella," he said. "I'm gonna gig him." He struck twice at the snake and missed.

"Estella," Anna said, "I saw his head. He can't go away. He's swallowed one of the fish. He's caught on the stringer." She shuddered with disgust. "What are we going to do?" she said. "Let's throw away the stringer. We'll never get him off."

"All them beautiful fish! No, *Ma'am*," Estella said. "Here, Ralph, he can't bite us if he's swallowed a fish. I'll untie the stringer and get him up on land, and then you gig him."

"I'm going away," Steve said. "I don't want to watch." He crossed the hill and went back to the beach, where he sat down alone and began to dig a hole in the sand.

Ralph, wild with excitement, danced impatiently around Estella while she untied the stringer.

"Be calm, child," she said. She pulled the stringer out of the water and dropped it on the ground. "Now!"

The snake had indeed tried to swallow one of the bream on the stringer. Its jaws were stretched so wide as to look dislocated; its body was distended behind the head with the half-swallowed meal, and the fish's head could still be seen protruding from its mouth. The snake, faintly banded with slaty black on a brown background, was a water moccasin.

"Lord, it's a cottonmouth!" Estella cried as soon as she had the stringer out on land, where she could see the snake.

A thrill of horror and disgust raised the hair on Anna's arms. The thought of the helpless fish on the stringer sensing its enemy's approach, and then of the snake, equally and even more grotesquely helpless, filled her with revulsion. "Throw it away," she commanded. And then the thought of the stringer with its living burden of fish and snake struggling and swimming away into the lake struck her as even worse. "No!" she said. "Go on. Kill the snake, Ralph."

Ralph paid no attention to his mother but stood with the long gig poised, looking up at Estella for instructions.

"Kill him," Estella said. "Now."

He drove the gig into the snake's body behind the head and pinned it to the ground, where it coiled and uncoiled convulsively, wrapping its tail around the gig and then unwrapping it and whipping it across the sand.

Anna mastered her horror as well as she could with a

shake of her head. "Now what?" she said calmly.

Estella got a knife from the tackle box, held the dead but still writhing snake down with one big foot behind the gig on its body and the other on its tail, squatted, and deftly cut off the fish's head where it protruded from the gaping, fanged mouth. Then she worked the barbed point of the gig out of the body, picked the snake up on the point, and stood holding it away from her.

Ralph whirled around with excitement and circled Estella twice. "We've killed a snake," he chanted. "We've killed a snake. We've killed a snake."

"Look at it wiggle," Murray said. "It keeps on wiggling even after it's dead."

"Yeah, a snake'll wiggle like that for an hour sometimes, even with its head cut off," Estella said. "Look out, Ralph." She swept the gig forward through the air and threw the snake out into the pool, where it continued its aimless writhing on the surface of the water. She handed Ralph the gig and stood watching the snake for a few minutes, holding her hands away from her sides to keep the blood off her clothes. Then she bent down by the water's edge and washed the blood from her hands. She picked up the stringer, dropped the fish into the water, and tied the stringer to the root of the cottonwood. "There!" she said. "I didn't have no idea of throwing away all them — *those* beautiful fish. James would've skinned me if he ever heard about it."

Steve got up from the sand now and came over to his mother. He looked at the wiggling snake, and then he leaned against his mother without saying anything, put his arms around her, and laid his head against her side.

Anna stroked his hair with one hand and held him against her with the other. "It was a moccasin, honey," she said. "They're poison, you know. You have to kill them."

"I'm hungry," Ralph said. "Is it time to eat?"

Anna shook her head, gave Steve a pat, and released him. "Let me smoke a cigarette first and forget about that old snake. Then we'll eat."

Anna and Estella went back to the shade on the hill and settled themselves once more, each with a fresh can of beer and a cigarette. The children returned to the beach.

"I can do without snakes," Anna said. "Indefinitely."

Estella was still breathing hard. "I don't mind killing no snake," she said happily.

"I never saw anything like that before," Anna said. "A snake getting caught on a stringer, I mean. Did you?"

"Once or twice," Estella said. "And I've had 'em get after my stringer plenty of times."

"I don't see how you could stand to cut the fish's head off," Anna said, and shivered.

"Well, somebody had to."

"Yes, I suppose I would have done it if you hadn't been here." She laughed. "Maybe. I was mighty tempted to throw the whole thing away."

"I'm just as glad I wasn't pregnant," Estella said. "I'm glad it didn't happen while I was carrying Lee Roy. I would have been *helpless*."

"You might have had a miscarriage," Anna said. She laughed again, still nervous, wanting to stop talking about the snake but not yet able to, feeling somehow that there was more to be said. "Please don't have any miscarriages on fishing trips with me," she went on. "I can do without that, too."

"Miscarriage!" Estella said. "That's not what I'm talking about. And that reminds me, what I was getting ready to tell you when we saw the snake. You know, I said I had something on my mind?"

"Uh-huh."

"You remember last summer when you weren't home that day, and that kid fell out of the tree in the yard, and all?"

"How could I forget it?" Anna said.

"You remember you spoke to me so heavy about it?

Why didn't I stay out in the yard with him until his mama got there, instead of leaving him laying on the ground like that, nobody with him but Ralph, and I told you I couldn't go out there to him — couldn't look at that kid with his leg broke, and all — and you didn't understand why?"

"Yes, I remember," Anna said.

"Well, I wanted to tell you I was *blameless*," Estella said. "I didn't want you to know it at the time, but I was pregnant. I *couldn't* go out there. It might have *marked* my child, don't you see? I might have bore a cripple."

"Oh, Estella! You don't believe that kind of foolishness, do you?" Anna said.

"Believe it? I've seen it happen," Estella said. "I know it's true." She was sitting on the fallen log, so that she towered above Anna, who had gone back to her place on the ground, leaning against the tree. Now Estella leaned forward with an expression of intense seriousness on her face. "My aunt looked on a two-headed calf when she was carrying a child," she said, "and her child had six fingers on one hand and seven on the other."

Anna hitched herself up higher, then got up and sat down on the log beside Estella. "But that was an accident," she said. "A coincidence. Looking at the calf didn't have anything to do with it."

Estella shook her head stubbornly. "This world is a mysterious place," she said. "Do you think you can understand everything in it?"

"No," Anna said. "Not everything. But I don't believe in magic."

"All this world is full of mystery," Estella repeated. "You got to have respect for what you don't understand. There are times to be brave and times when you go down helpless in spite of all. Like that snake. You were afraid of that snake."

"I thought he might bite me," Anna said. "And besides, it was so horrible the way he was caught."

But Estella went on as if she hadn't heard. "You see,"

she said, "there are things you overlook. Things, like I was telling you about my aunt, that are *true*. My mother in her day saw more wonders than that. She knew more than one that sickened and died of a spell. And this child with the fingers, I know about him for a fact. I lived with them when I was teaching school. I lived in the house with that kid. So I'm not taking any chances."

"But I thought you had lost your head and got scared because he was hurt," Anna said. "When the little boy broke his leg, I mean. I kept thinking it wasn't like you. That's what really happened, isn't it?"

"No," Estella said. "It was like I told you."

Anna said no more, but sat quiet a long time, lighting another cigarette and smoking calmly, her face expressionless. But her thoughts were in a tumult of exasperation, bafflement, and outrage. She tried unsuccessfully to deny, to block out, the overriding sense of the difference between herself and Estella, borne in on her by this strange conversation so foreign to their quiet, sensible friendship. She had often thought, with pride both in herself and in Estella, what an accomplishment their friendship was, knowing how much delicacy of feeling, how much consideration and understanding they had both brought to it. And now it seemed to her that it was this very friendship, so carefully nurtured for years, that Estella had unwittingly attacked. With a few words, she had put between them all that separated them, all the dark and terrible past. In the tumult of Anna's feelings there rose a queer, long-forgotten memory of a nurse she had once had as a child — the memory of a brown hand thrust out at her, holding a greasy black ball of hair combings. "You see, child, I saves my hair. I ain't never th'owed away a hair of my head."

"Why?" she had asked.

"Bad luck to th'ow away combings. Bad luck to lose any part of yourself in this old world. Fingernail parings, too. I gathers them up and carries them home and burns them. And I sits by the fire and watches until every last little bitty hair is turned plumb to smoke."

"But why?" she had asked again.

"Let your enemy possess one hair of your head and you will be in his power," the nurse had said. She had thrust the hair ball into her apron pocket, and now, in the memory, she seemed to be brushing Anna's hair, and Anna remembered standing restive under her hand, hating, as always, to have her hair brushed.

"Hurry up," she had said. "Hurry up. I got to go."

"All right, honey. I'm through." The nurse had given her head one last lick and then, bending toward her, still holding her arm while she struggled to be off and outdoors again, had thrust a dark, brooding face close to hers, had looked at her for a long, scary moment, and had laughed. "I saves your combings, too, honey. You in my power."

With an effort, Anna drew herself up short. She put out her cigarette, threw her beer can into the lake, and stood up. "I reckon we better fix some lunch," she said. "The children are starving."

By the time they had finished lunch, burned the discarded papers, thrown the bread crusts and crumbs of potato chips to the birds, and put the empty soft-drink bottles back in the cooler, it had begun to look like rain. Anna stood gazing thoughtfully into the sky. "Maybe we ought to start back," she said. "We don't want to get caught in the rain up here."

"We're not going to catch any more fish as long as the wind is blowing," Estella said.

"We want to swim some more," Ralph said.

"You can't go swimming right after lunch," Anna said. "You might get a cramp. And it won't be any fun to get caught in the rain. We'd better call it a day." She picked up one of the poles and began to wind the line around it. "Come on, kids," she said. "Let's load up."

They loaded their gear into the skiff and dropped the

and Steve to sit in the bow, facing the stern. Estella got in
cautiously and took the middle seat. Anna and Ralph
waded in together, pushed the skiff off the sandbar, and
then got into the stern.
"You all got your life jackets on?" Anna said, glancing
at the boys. "That's right."
Ralph pulled on the recoil-starter rope until he had got
the little motor started, and they headed down the lake.
The heavily loaded skiff showed no more than eight
inches of freeboard, and as they cut through the choppy
water, waves sprayed over the bow and sprinkled
Murray and Steve. Anna moved the tiller and headed the
skiff in closer to the shore. "We'll stay close in going
down," she said. "Water's not so rough in here. And then
we can cut across the lake right opposite the Yacht Club."
Estella sat still in the middle of the skiff, her back to
Anna, a hand on each gunwale, as they moved steadily
down the lake, rocking with the wind-rocked waves. "I
don't like this old lake when it's windy," Estella said. "I
don't like no windy water."
When they reached a point opposite the Yacht Club,
where the lake was a little more than a mile wide, Anna
headed the skiff into the rougher open water. The wind,
however, was still no more than a stiff breeze, and the
skiff was a quarter of the way across the lake before
Anna began to be worried. Spray from the choppy waves
was coming in more and more often over the bow; Murray
and Steve were drenched, and an inch of water sloshed in
the bottom of the skiff. Estella had not spoken since she
had said "I don't like no windy water." She sat perfectly
still, gripping the gunwales with both hands, her paper
sack of tackle in her lap, her worm can on the seat beside
her. Suddenly a gust of wind picked up the paper sack
and blew it out of the boat. It struck the water and floated
back to Anna, who reached out, picked it up, and dropped
it by her own feet. Estella did not move, although the
sack brushed against her face as it blew out. She made no

attempt to catch it. She's scared, Anna thought. She's so scared she didn't even see it blow away. And Anna was frightened herself. She leaned forward, picked up the worm can from the seat beside Estella, dumped out the worms and dirt, and tapped Estella on the shoulder. "Here," she said. "Why don't you bail some of the water out of the bottom of the boat, so your feet won't get wet?"

Estella did not look around, but reached over her shoulder, took the can, and began to bail, still holding to the gunwale tightly with her left hand.

The wind freshened, the waves began to show white at their tips, the clouds in the south raced across the sky, darker and darker. But still, although they could see sheets of rain far away to the south, the sun shone on them brightly. They were now almost halfway across the lake. Anna looked over her shoulder toward the quieter water they had left behind. Along the shore of the lake, the willow trees tossed in the wind like a forest of green plumes. It's just as far one way as the other, she thought, and anyhow there's nothing to be afraid of. But while she looked back, the boat slipped off course, no longer quartering the waves, and immediately they took a big one over their bow.

"Bail, Estella," Anna said quietly, putting the boat back on course. "Get that water out of the boat." Her mind was filled with one paralyzing thought: She can't swim. My God, Estella can't swim.

Far off down the channel she saw the *Gay Rosey Jane* moving steadily toward the terminal, pushing a string of barges. She looked at Murray and Steve in the bow of the boat, drenched, hair plastered to their heads. "Just sit still, boys," she said. "There's nothing to worry about. We're almost there."

The wind was a gale now, and the black southern sky rushed toward them as if to engulf them. The boat took another wave over the bow, and then another. Estella bailed mechanically with the coffee can. They were still almost half a mile out from the Yacht Club. The boat's overloaded, and we're going to sink, Anna thought. My God, we're going to sink, and Estella can't swim.

"Estella," she said, "the boat will not sink. It may fill up with water, but it won't sink. Do you understand? It is all filled with cork, like a life preserver. It won't sink, do you hear me?" She repeated herself louder and louder above the wind. Estella sat with her back turned and bailed. She did not move or answer, or even nod her head. She went on bailing frantically, mechanically, dumping pint after pint of water over the side while they continued to ship waves over the bow. Murray and Steve sat in their places and stared at Anna. Ralph sat motionless by her side. No one said a word. I've got to take care of them all, Anna thought. Estella kept on bailing. The boat settled in the water and shipped another wave, wallowing now, hardly moving before the labored push of the motor. Estella gave a yell and started to rise, holding to the gunwales with both hands.

"Sit down, you fool!" Anna shouted. *"Sit down!"*

"We're gonna sink!" Estella yelled. "And I can't swim, Miss Anna! I can't swim!" For the first time, she turned, and stared at Anna with wild, blind eyes. She stood all the way up and clutched the air. "I'm gonna drown!" she yelled.

The boat rocked and settled, the motor drowned out, another wave washed in over the bow, and the boat tipped slowly up on its side. An instant later, they were all in the water and the boat was floating upside down beside them.

The children bobbed up immediately, buoyant in their life jackets. Anna glanced around once to see if they were all there. "Stay close to the boat, boys," she said.

And then Estella heaved out of the water, fighting frantically, eyes vacant, mouth open, the broad expanse of her golden face set in mindless desperation.

Anna got hold of one of the handgrips at the stern of the boat and, with her free hand, grabbed Estella's arm. "You're all right," she said. "Come on, I've got hold of the boat."

She tried to pull the huge bulk of the Negro woman toward her and guide her hand to the grip. Estella did not speak, but lunged forward in the water with a strangled yell and threw herself on Anna, flinging her arms across her shoulders. Anna felt herself sinking and scissors-kicked strongly to keep herself up, but she went down. Chin-deep in the water, she threw back her head and took a breath before Estella pushed her under. She hung on to the grip with all her strength, feeling herself battered against the boat and jerked away from it by Estella's struggle. This can't be happening, she thought. We can't be out here drowning. She felt a frantic hand brush across her face and snatch at her nose and hair. My glasses, she thought as she felt them torn away. I've lost my glasses.

Estella's weight slid away, and she, too, went under. Then both women came up and Anna got hold of Estella's arm again. "Come *on*," she gasped. "The *boat*."

Again Estella threw herself forward, the water streaming from her head and shoulders. This time Anna pulled her close enough to get hold of the grip, but Estella did not try to grasp it. Her hand slid, clawing, along Anna's wrist and arm; again she somehow rose up in the water and came down on Anna, and again the two women went under. This time, Estella's whole thrashing bulk was above Anna; she held with all her strength to the handgrip, but felt herself torn away from it. She came up behind Estella, who was now clawing frantically at the side of the skiff which sank down on their side and tipped gently toward them as she pulled at it.

Anna ducked down and somehow got her shoulder against Estella's rump. Kicking and heaving with a strength she did not possess, she boosted Estella up and forward so that she fell sprawling across the boat. "*There!*" She came up as the rocking skiff began to submerge under Estella's weight. "*Stay* there!" she gasped. "*Stay* on it. For God's . . ."

But the boat was under a foot of water now, rocking

and slipping away under Estella's shifting weight. Clutching and kicking crazily, mouth open in a soundless prolonged scream, eyes staring, she slipped off the other side, turned her face toward Anna, gave a strange, strangled grunt, and sank again. The water churned and foamed where she had been.

Anna swam around the boat toward her. As she swam, she realized that Ralph and Steve were screaming for help. Murray floated in the water with a queer, embarrassed smile on his face, as if he had been caught at something shameful. "I'm not here," he seemed to be saying. "This is all just an embarrassing mistake."

By the time Anna got to Estella, the boat was a couple of yards away — too far, she knew, for her to try to get Estella back to it. Estella broke the surface of the water directly in front of her and immediately flung both arms around her neck. Nothing Anna had ever learned in a lifesaving class seemed to have any bearing on this reasonless two hundred pounds of flesh with which she had to deal. They went down. This time they stayed under so long, deep in the softly yielding black water, that Anna thought she would not make it back up. Her very brain seemed ready to burst out of her ears and nostrils. She scissors-kicked again and again with all her strength — not trying to pull loose from Estella's clinging but now more passive weight — and they came up. Anna's head was thrust up and back, ready for a breath, and the instant she felt the air on her face, she took it, deep and gulping, swallowing some water at the same time, and they went down again. Estella's arms rested heavily — trustingly, it seemed — on her shoulders. She did not hug Anna or try to strangle her but simply kept holding on and pushing her down. This time, again deep in the dark water, when Anna raised her arms for a strong downstroke, she touched a foot. One of the boys was floating above their heads. She grabbed the foot without a thought and pulled with all her strength, scissors-kicking at the same time. She and Estella popped out of the water. Gasping in the life-giving air, Anna found herself staring into Steve's face as he floated beside her, weeping.

My God, I'll drown him if he doesn't get out of the way, she thought. I'll drown my own child. But she had no time to say even a word to warn him off before they went down again.

The next time up, she heard Ralph's voice, high and shrill and almost in her ear, and realized that he, too, was swimming close by, and was pounding on Estella's shoulder. "Estella, let go, let go!" he was crying. "Estella, you're drowning Mama!" Estella did not hear. She seemed not even to try to raise her head or breathe when their heads broke out of the water.

Once more they went under and came up before Anna thought, I've given out. There's no way to keep her up, and nobody is coming. And then, deep in the lake, the brassy taste of fear on her tongue, the yielding water pounding in her ears: *She's going to drown me. I've got to let her drown, or she will drown me.* She drew her knee up under her chin, planted her foot in the soft belly, still swollen from pregnancy, and shoved as hard as she could, pushing herself up and back and Estella down and away. Estella was not holding her tightly, and it was easy to push her away. The big arms slid off Anna's shoulders, the limp hands making no attempt to clutch or hold.

They had been together, close as lovers in the darkness or as twins in the womb of the lake, and now they were apart. Anna shot up into the air with the force of her shove and took a deep, gasping breath. Treading water, she waited for Estella to come up beside her, but nothing happened. The three children floated in a circle and looked at her. A vision passed through her mind of Estella's body drifting downward, downward through layers of increasing darkness, all her golden strength and flowery beauty mud-and-water-dimmed, still, aimless as a drifting log. I ought to surface-dive and look for her, she thought, and the thought of going down again turned her bowels to water.

Before she had to decide to dive, something nudged lightly against her hand, like an inquiring, curious fish. She grabbed at it and felt the inert mass of Estella's body, drained of struggle, floating below the surface of the water. She got hold of the belt of her dress and pulled. Estella's back broke the surface of the water, mounded and rocking in the dead man's float, and then sank gently down again. Anna held on to the belt. She moved her feet tiredly to keep herself afloat and looked around her. I can't even get her face out of the water, she thought. I haven't the strength to lift her head.

The boat was floating ten yards away. The Skotch cooler, bright red-and-black plaid, bobbed gaily in the water nearby. Far, far off she could see the levee. In the boat it had looked so near and the distance across the lake so little that she had said she could easily swim it, but now everything in the world except the boat, the children, and this lifeless body was unthinkably far away. Tiny black figures moved back and forth along the levee, people going about their business without a thought of tragedy. The whole sweep of the lake was empty, with not another boat in sight except the *Gay Rosey Jane*, still moving up the channel. All that had happened had happened so quickly that the towboat seemed no nearer than it had before the skiff overturned. Murray floated in the water a few yards off, still smiling his embarrassed smile. Steve and Ralph stared at their mother with stricken faces. The sun broke through the shifting blackness of the sky, and at the same time a light rain began to fall, pattering on the choppy surface of the lake and splashing into their faces.

All her senses dulled and muffled by shock and exhaustion, Anna moved her feet and worked her way toward the boat, dragging her burden.

"She's gone," Steve said. "Estella's drowned." Tears

and rain streamed down his face.

"What shall we do, Mama?" Ralph said.

Dimly, Anna realized that he had sensed her exhaustion and was trying to rouse her.

"Yell," she said. "All three of you yell. Maybe somebody ..."

The children screamed for help again and again, their thin, piping voices floating away on the wind. With her last strength, Anna continued to work her way toward the boat, pulling Estella after her. She swam on her back, frog-kicking, and feeling the inert bulk bump against her legs at every stroke. When she reached the boat, she took hold of the handgrip and concentrated on holding on to it.

"What shall we do?" Ralph said again. "They can't hear us."

Overcome with despair, Anna let her head droop toward the water. "No one is coming," she said. "It's too far. They can't hear you." And then, from somewhere, dim thoughts of artificial respiration, of snatching back the dead, came into her mind and she raised her head. Still time. I've got to get her out *now*, she thought. "Yell again," she said.

"I'm going to swim to shore and get help," Ralph said. He looked toward his mother for a decision, but his face clearly showed that he knew he could not expect one. He started swimming away, his blond head bobbing in the rough water. He did not look back.

"I don't know," Anna said. Then she remembered vaguely that in an accident you were supposed to stay with the boat. "She's dead," she said to herself. "My God, she's dead. My fault."

Ralph swam on, the beloved head smaller and smaller on the vast expanse of the lake. The *Gay Rosey Jane* moved steadily up the channel. They might run him down, Anna thought. They'd never see him. She opened her mouth to call him back.

"Somebody's coming!" Murray shouted. "They see us. Somebody's coming. Ralph!"

Ralph heard him and turned back, and now they saw two boats racing toward them, one from the Yacht Club and one from the far side of the lake, across from the terminal. In the nearer one they saw Gaines Williamson.

Thirty yards away, something happened to Gaines's engine; it raced, ground, and died. Standing in the stern of the rocking boat, he worked frantically over it while they floated and watched. It could not have been more than a minute or two before the other boat pulled up beside them, but every moment that passed, Anna knew, might be the moment of Estella's death. In the stern of the second boat they saw a wiry white man wearing a T-shirt and jeans. He cut his engine when he was beside them, and, moving quickly to the side of the boat near Anna, bent over her in great excitement. "Are you all right?" he asked. He grabbed her arm with a hard, calloused hand and shook her as if he had seen that she was about to pass out. "Are you all right?" he asked again, his face close to hers.

Anna stared at him, scarcely understanding what the question meant. The children swam over to the boat, and he helped them in and then turned back to Anna. "Come on," he said, and took hold of her arm again. "You've got to help yourself. Can you make it?"

"Get this one first," she said.

"What?" He stared at her with a queer, concentrated gaze, and she realized that he had not even seen Estella.

She hauled on the belt, and Estella's back broke the surface of the water, rolling, rocking, and bumping against the side of the boat. "I've got somebody else here," she said.

He grunted as if someone had hit him in the stomach. Reaching down he grabbed the back of Estella's dress, pulled her toward him, got one hand into her hair, raised her face out of the water, and, bracing himself against the gunwale, held her there. Estella's peaceful face turned slowly toward him. Her mouth and eyes were closed, her expression was one of deep repose. The man stared at her and then at Anna. "My God," he said.

"We've got to get her into the boat," Anna said. "If we can get her where we can give her artificial respiration . . ."

"It's Estella," Steve said. "Mama had her all the time." He began to cry again. "Let go of her hair," he said. "You're hurting her."

The three children shifted all at once to the side of the boat where the man was still holding Estella, and he turned on them sternly. "Get back," he said. "Sit *down*. And sit still."

The children scuttled back to their places. "You're hurting her," Steve said again.

"It's all right, son," the man said. "She can't feel a thing." To Anna, in a lower voice, he said, "She's dead."

"I'll push and you pull," Anna said. "Maybe we can get her into the boat."

He shifted his position, bracing himself as well as he could in the rocking boat, rested Estella's head on his own shoulder, and put both arms around her. They heaved and pushed at the limp body, but they could not get her into the boat. The man let her down in to the water again, this time holding her under the arms. A hundred yards away, Gaines still struggled with his engine.

"Hurry up!" the man shouted. "Get on over here. We can't lift this woman by ourselves."

"Fishing lines tangled in the screw!" Gaines shouted back. His engine caught and died again.

"We're going to have to tow her in," the man said. "That fellow can't start his boat." He reached behind him and got a life jacket. "We'd better put this on her," he said. They worked Estella's arms into the life jacket and fastened the straps. "I've got a rope here somewhere," he said. "Hold her a minute. Wait." He handed Anna a life jacket. "You put one on, too." While he still held Estella by the hair, Anna struggled into the life jacket, and then took hold of the straps of Estella's. Just then, Gaines got his engine started, raced across the open water, and drew up beside them.

The two boats rocked in the rough water with Anna and Estella between them. Anna, with a hand on the gunwale of each, held them apart while the two men, straining and grunting, hauled Estella's body up out of the water and over the gunwale of Gaines's boat. Gaines heaved her legs in. She flopped, face down, across the seat and lay with one arm hanging over the side, the hand trailing in the water. Anna lifted the arm and put it in the boat. Then the white man pulled Anna into his boat. As he helped her over the side, she heard a smacking blow, and, looking back, saw that Gaines had raised and turned Estella's body and was pounding her in the belly. Water poured out of her mouth and, in reflex, air rushed in.

The boats roared off across the lake toward the Yacht Club. The white man's was much the faster of the two, and he quickly pulled away. As soon as they were within calling distance, he stood up in the boat and began to yell at the little group gathered on the Yacht Club mooring float. "Drowned! She's drowned!" he yelled. "Call an ambulance. Get a resuscitator down here. Hurry!"

They drew up to the float. He threw a rope to one of the Negroes standing there and jumped out. Anna dragged herself to a sitting position and stared stupidly at the crowd of Negroes. Gaines Williamson pulled up behind them in the other boat.

"Give us a hand," the white man said. "Let's get her out of there. My God, she's huge. Somebody lend a hand."

To Anna it seemed that all the rest of the scene on the float took place above and far away from her. She saw legs moving back and forth, heard voices and snatches of conversation, felt herself moved from one place to another, but nothing that happened interrupted her absorption in grief and guilt. For the time, nothing existed for her except the belief that Estella was dead.

155

Someone took her arm and helped her onto the float while the children climbed up by themselves. She sat down on the splintery boards, surrounded by legs, and no one paid any attention to her.

"I saw 'em." The voice of a Negro woman in the crowd. "I was setting on the levee and I saw 'em. You heard me. 'My Lord save us, some folks out there drowning,' I said. I was up on the levee and I run down to the Yacht Club . . ."

"Did somebody call an ambulance?" the white man asked.

"I run down here to the Yacht Club, like to killed myself running, and . . ."

"How . . ."

"*Gay Rosey Jane* swamped them. Never even seen them. Them towboats don't stop for nobody. See, there she goes. Never seen them at all."

"Still got a stitch in my side. My Lord, I liked to killed myself running."

"Anybody around here know how to give artificial respiration?"

"I was sitting right yonder on the terminal fishing with her this morning. Would you believe that?"

"God have mercy on us."

"Oh, Lord. Oh, Lord God. Lord God."

"Have mercy on us."

A young Negro in Army khakis walked over to where the white man and Gaines Williamson were trying to get Estella out of the bulky jacket. "We'll cut it off," he said calmly. He pulled a straight razor from his pocket, slit one shoulder of the life jacket, pushed it out of the way, and straddled Estella's body. "I know how," he said. "I learned in the Army." He arranged her body in position — lying flat on her stomach, face turned to the side and arms above her head — and set to work, raising her arms and then her body rhythmically. When he lifted her body in the middle, her face dragged on the splintery planks of the float.

Anna crawled through the crowd to where Estella lay.

Squatting down without a word, she put her hands under Estella's face to protect it from the splinters. It passed through her mind that she should do something about the children. Looking around, she saw them standing in a row at one side of the float, staring down at her and Estella — no longer crying, just standing and staring. Somebody ought to get them away from here, she thought vaguely, but the thought left her mind and she forgot them. She swayed, rocked back on her heels, sat down suddenly, and then lay on her stomach, her head against Estella's head, her hands cradling the sleeping face.

Who's going to tell James, she thought. Who's going to tell him she's dead? And then, I. I have to tell him. She began to talk to Estella. "Please, darling," she said. "Please, Estella, breathe." Tears of weakness rolled down her face, and she looked up above the forest of legs at the black faces in a circle around them. "She's got four babies," she said. "*Babies.* Who's going to tell her husband she's dead? Who's going to tell him?" And then, again, "Please, Estella, breathe. Please breathe."

No one answered. The young Negro soldier continued to raise the limp arms and body alternately, his motions deliberate and rhythmical, the sweat pouring off his face and dripping down on his sweat-soaked shirt. His thin face was intent and stern. The storm was over, the clouds to the west had blown away, and the sun had come out and beat down bright and hot, raising steamy air from the rain-soaked float.

A long time passed. The soldier giving Estella artificial respiration looked around at the crowd. "Anybody know how to do this? I'm about to give out." He did not pause or break the rhythm of his motions.

A man stepped out of the crowd. "I can do it," he said. "I know how."

"Come on, then," the soldier said. "Get down here by me and do it with me three times, and then, when I stop, you take over. Don't break it."

"Please, Estella," Anna said. "Please."

"One . . . Two . . . "

She felt someone pulling at her arm and looked up. A policeman was standing over her. "Here, lady," he said. "Get up off that dock. You ain't doing no good."

"But the splinters will get in her face," Anna said. "I'm holding her face off the boards."

"It ain't going to matter if her face is tore up if she's dead," the policeman said. "Get up."

Someone handed her a towel, and she folded it and put it under Estella's face. The policeman dragged her to her feet and took her over to a chair near the edge of the float and sat her down in it. He squatted beside her. "Now, who was in the boat?" he said. "I got to make a report."

Anna made a vague gesture. "We were," she said.

"Who is 'we,' lady?"

"Estella and I and the children."

"Lady, give me the names, please," the policeman said.

"Estella Moseby, the Negro woman. She used to work for me and we *asked* her, we asked her — " She broke off.

"Come on, who else?"

Anna stared at him, a short, bald man with shining pink scalp, and drum belly buttoned tightly into his uniform. A wave of nausea overcame her, and she saw his head surrounded by the shimmering black spokes of a rimless wheel, a black halo. "I'm going to be sick," she said. Collapsing out of the chair onto the dock, she leaned her head over the edge and vomited into the lake.

He waited until she was through and then helped her back into her chair. "Who else was with you?" he said.

"My two children, Ralph and Steve," she said. "Murray McCrae. I am Mrs. Richard Glover."

"Where is this McCrae fellow? He all right?"

"He's a little *boy*," Anna said. "A child. He's over there somewhere."

"You sure there wasn't nobody else with you?"

"No. That's all," Anna said.

"Now, give me the addresses, please. Where did the nigger live?"

"For God's sake," Anna said. "What difference does it make? Go away and let me alone."

"I got to make my report, lady."

Ralph tugged at Anna's arm. "Mama, hadn't I better call Daddy?" he said.

"Yes," she said. "Yes, I guess you had." Oh, God, she thought, he has to find out. I can't put it off. Everybody has to find out that Estella is dead.

Anna heard a commotion on the levee. The steadily increasing crowd separated, and two white-jacketed men appeared and began to work over Estella. Behind them, a woman with a camera snapped pictures.

"What are they taking *pictures* of her for?" Anna asked.

Then she heard her husband's voice shouting, "Get off the damn raft, God damn it! Get off. You want to sink it? Get back there. You want to drown us all?"

The policeman stood up and went toward the crowd. "What the hell?" Anna heard him say.

"And put that camera up, if you don't want me to throw it in the lake." Anna's husband was in a fury of outrage, and concentrated it for the moment on the woman reporter from the local newspaper, who was snapping pictures of Estella.

"You all right, Anna?" Richard asked her.

The people on the float were scuttling back to the levee, and the reporter had disappeared. Anna, who was still sitting where the policeman had left her, nodded, and opened her mouth to speak, but her husband was gone before she could say anything. She felt a wave of self-pity. He didn't even stay to help me, she thought.

Then, a moment or an hour later — she did not know how long — she heard a strange high-pitched shriek from the other end of the float. What's that, she thought. It sounded again — a long, rasping rattle and then a shriek. Does the machine they brought make that queer noise?

"She's breathing," somebody said.

"No," Anna said aloud to nobody, for nobody was listening. "No. She's dead. I couldn't help it. I let her drown. Who's going to tell James?"

The float was cleared now. Besides Estella and Anna, only the two policemen, the two men from the ambulance, and Gaines Williamson were on it. The man who had rescued them was gone. The crowd stood quietly on the levee.

"Where is Richard?" Anna said. "Did he leave?"

No one answered.

The long, rasping rattle and shriek sounded again. Gaines Williamson came over to where Anna was sitting, and bent down to her, smiling kindly. "She's alive, Mrs. Glover," he said. "She's going to be all right."

Anna shook her head.

"Yes, ma'am. She's moving and breathing, and yelling like crazy. She's going to be all right."

Anna got up shakily. She walked over to where the men were working Estella onto a stretcher.

"What's she doing?" she said. "What's the matter with her?"

Estella was thrashing her arms and legs furiously, mouth open, eyes staring, her face again the mask of mindless terror that Anna had seen in the lake. The rattle and shriek were her breathing and screaming.

"She must think she's still in the water," one of the men said. "Shock. But she's O.K. Look at her kick."

Anna sat down on the float, her knees buckling under her, and someone pulled her out of the way while four men carried the stretcher off the float and up the levee toward the ambulance.

Richard reappeared at the foot of the levee and crossed the walkway to the Yacht Club float. He bent down to help her up. "I'm sorry I had to leave you," he said. "I had to get the children away from here and find someone to take them home."

"My God," Anna said. "She's alive. They said she would be all right."

Later, in the car, she said to her husband, "She kept

pushing me down, Richard. I tried to hold her up, I tried to make her take hold of the boat. But she kept pushing me down."

"It's all right now," he said. "Try not to think about it any more."

The next day, when Anna visited Estella in the hospital, she learned that Estella remembered almost nothing of what had happened. She recalled getting into the skiff for the trip home, but everything after that was gone.

"James says you saved my life," she said, in a hoarse whisper, "and I thank you."

Her husband stood at the head of her bed, gray-haired and dignified in his Sunday suit. He nodded. "The day won't come when we'll forget it, Miss Anna," he said. "God be my witness."

Anna shook her head. "I never should have taken you out without a life preserver," she said.

"Ain't she suppose to be a grown woman?" James said. "She suppose to know better herself."

"How do you feel?" Anna asked.

"Lord, not a square inch on my body don't ache," Estella said. She laid her hands on the mound of her body under the sheet. "My stomach!" she said, with a wry laugh. "Somebody must've jumped up and down on it."

"I reckon that's from the artificial respiration," Anna said. "I had never seen anyone do it that way before. They pick you up under the stomach and then put you down and lift your arms. And then, too, I kicked you. And we must have banged you up some getting you into the boat. Lord! The more I think about it, the worse it gets. Because Gaines hit you in the stomach, too, as soon as he got you into the boat. That's what really saved your life. As soon as he got you into the boat, he hit you in the stomach and got rid of a lot of the water in your lungs and let in some air. I believe that breath you took in Gaines's boat kept you alive until we got you to the dock."

"You kicked me?" Estella said.

"We were going down," Anna said, feeling that she must confess to Estella the enormity of what she had done, "and I finally knew I couldn't keep you up. I kicked you in the stomach hard, and got loose from you, and then when you came up I grabbed you and held on, and about that time they saw us and the boats came. You passed out just when I kicked you, or else the kick knocked you out, because you didn't struggle any more. I reckon that was lucky, too."

Estella shook her head. "I can't remember anything about it," she whispered. "Not anything." She pointed out the window toward the smokestack rising from the opposite wing of the hospital. "Seems like last night I got the idea there's a little man up there," she said. "He peeps out from behind the smokestack at me, and I'm afraid of him. He leans on the smokestack, and then he jumps away real quick, like it's hot, and one time he came right over here and stood on the window ledge and looked in at me. Lucky the window was shut. I said 'Boo!' and, you know, he fell off! It didn't hurt him; he came right back. He wants to tell me something, yes, but he can't get in." She closed her eyes.

Anna looked anxiously at James.

"They still giving her something to keep her quiet," he said. "Every so often she gets a notion somebody trying to get in here."

Estella opened her eyes. "I thank you, Miss Anna," she said. "James told me you saved my life." She smiled. "Seems like every once in a while I hear your voice," she said. "Way off. Way, way off. You're saying, 'I'll save you, Estella. Don't be afraid. I'll save you.' That's all I can remember."

Jesus Knew

E.P. O'DONNELL

The Mississippi had clawed through its west bank. Alert
boatmen were paddling about finding people marooned.
Refugee camps had sprung up here and there, clusters of
pointed tents the color of the river, standing like military
encampments without arms or colors.

In the shriveled hamlet of Tête Noir there was one living person — a girl in a magnolia tree with a milk goat.
The tree was full of white flowers the size of a baby's
head. The goat straddled a branch, and the girl held her
by the horn. All around them below was the thick yellow
water, hardly flowing. All morning they sat there, and
the goat made frantic attempts to reach the leaves above
her head. The girl wore a silver star hanging on a string
from her neck.

In the afternoon the girl was crying out, "Jesus! Jesus!"
She looked like a pale Indian — the inscrutable eyes and
the opulent braids of hair dangling. She was groggy with
hunger. The rough bark bit deeply into the crook of her

arm. The goat kicked violently. After calling Jesus for the last time she heard the brittle rapping of an approaching motorboat with voices. Then she thanked Jesus and waited.

The two men in the boat were volunteer rescuers, both very dark, of uncertain racial stock. Airplane scouts had reported some refugees marooned in the attic of Bubber Joe's, a large cotton gin south of Tête Noir. The men turned their faces about and about, searching. A cotton gin is a fat gray-hided mass of timbers with four thick legs and a pendant metal trunk, to inhale in a few moments the product of an entire family's labor for a year.

"You smell the mules?" asked Ed Jefferson, the one in charge. "Tell me Bayou Desjardins is chocked up with big dead sugar mules."

"I don't see no cotton gin," said Pauly, his companion.

No one was about to direct them. The town was under water twelve feet. The consolidated school, its lower floor submerged, squatted in the bright yellow silence with a limp flag on the tall staff.

"I thought the schoolhouse'd be fulla pretty teachers," said Ed, "leanin' out the windows to be saved."

A faint call was heard, the girl in the distant magnolia. They swung their boat round, cutting through the school-yard. The boat sent waves over the tops of the two basketball goals. Ed Jefferson was a good mechanic and a boatman. On the bows of his boat he had painted in white lead the name: HOT SHOT SAVIOR.

They found the girl. Her eyes were swollen and glad, but rather incredulous. "Hurry, she's fixin' to fall," said Pauly. Jefferson began to yodel:

"O de ole lady!
De ole lady who-o-o-o-o!"

They made fast to the tree and took in the girl and her goat.

"Thanksa," she murmured and sat on a bench, sedately pulling down her skirts and folding her tan hands in her lap, her thoughts far astray. The goat slipped about in the boat, uttering its soft dainty *meh-eh-eh-eh-eh!* and falling to its knees when a sharp turn was made among the chimneys.

"Better be milkin' that nanny!" Ed shouted. "She's leakin' on you! Where's your folks at, Brown?" Ed was always hoping they would rescue a girl whose father and brothers had been drowned.

"Cross de river, I reckonsa," she answered in a faraway tone. She held the goat by the horn and softly caressed its wet rump. She looked straight ahead, whispering, "Jesus knew! Jesus knew!"

Ed tossed her the rusty bailing can, and she milked without a word. Ed craned his neck to see into the pocket of her lowered bosom. Pauly kept examining the lush treetops where melancholy hens peered through the leaves. Pauly was an old man.

"Say where do you aim to go from here?" Ed shouted to the girl. "The Delta Arms Hotel, I reckon." He was about nineteen, with mischievous eyes. The girl looked up, and her soft eyes widened. On her still whispering lips a mechanical smile came, then died. She started milking again and thanking Jesus. Ed winked to Pauly.

"Hey, Brown!" Ed yelled. "Tell us where you think you goin'!"

"Don't knowsa," the girl responded without looking up. "Some place dry, I reckonsa, if yous de Raid Cross."

Ed dragged a comb through his frizzly hair and wiped the engine. They could tell how the streets were laid out by the ranks of roofs, each roof making a V-shaped rift in the water, creating the illusion in the stillness that the water was stationary and the roofs moved north in unison.

"You goin' some place dry, all right!" Ed bellowed.

"Gooden dry," said Pauly.

Ed said, "You know where we're fixin' to take you? Over the river to the convict camp. You know what convicts is? That's them bad, bad rascals with the striped laigs, come from under the jail to bag the levee."

The girl looked at Ed, for the first time actually attentive. She had rather proud lips and breasts — young, with clear-eyed gravity in her face of a recent successful baptism.

"They needin' somebody to cook their greens over there," Ed went on casually now, "an' wash them striped britches. Warden say, 'Find me a willin' an' a pretty girl ain't scared of convicts, because my gun robbers is gettin' hongry and lonesome at night in these tents atop of the levee.' Yare! We been lookin' for you all day, Brown. They ain't goin' to hit you in that camp. Not a nice girl like you. What's your name?"

"Ella McCoy."

"Why, that's a drudge. She named after a drudge boat, Pauly!"

The girl watched Ed's serious face. She was weeping inside. There was no change in her expression except the big globular tears hanging in the sun.

"Mind out where you're steerin', Ed!" Pauly warned.

"Listen, lil nigger, he's only jokin' you!"

Ed chuckled richly and stamped his feet. The girl dumped her can of milk over the side and began to sob pitifully. Ed's eyes grew kind.

"Now I'll tell you *sho-nuff* where you goin'!" said Ed. "You goin' to the big ark, an' see the lights from Baton Rouge and smell the refinery, and you eat you some boar jowl and clabber. Git you a pretty new refugee dress an' some typhoid serums. You love boar jowl?"

"Yassa."

"Fair enough."

They ducked their heads to pass under some telephone wires. A boat went by with a man grinding a camera at them; and one of its occupants shouted to Ed that the Bubber Joe refugees had been brought in.

Ed's boat curved out into the true river. On the big lonely river, whose turbulence the crevasse had

strangely allayed, it was a glorious rosy evening. Their
engine spat a nice row of vapor balls, exactly spaced, that
remained fixed behind them for a long time, reddened by
sun. The east shore lay free from water, calm russet fields
melting out into the horizon's bluish haze. And hunched
gleaners crept there among the pale strips of lettuce, all
heedless of the flood across the way, as if they did not
yet know.

Ed said to the girl, "Now you find you somebody on the
ark to mind your goat tonight like a good girl. We don't
want to be bothered by no nanny goat when we walk
down the dark levee, me and you."

The girl, jerked from a reverie, looked up quickly, then
lowered her eyes, regarding her folded hands. "Yassa,"
she answered.

"You understan' now, Brown? You goin' to treat me
white?"

The girl stroked the goat.

"Looka here, Brown!" She looked at him. He asked,
"Who was it save your life an' you was fixin' to fall in the
tree yonder? Did you ever seen me before?"

"I see you to de fillin' station in town, Cunnel Jessup
Fillin' Station."

"Correct! Now who was it save your life yonder?"

Part of a baseball park fence passed, then some sodden
bags of oats waltzing slowly and sprouting oats through
the seams. Ed contemplated the floating baseball score-
board lazily. "Tell me who done that, Brown? An' who
save you from the striped-laigged convicts?"

"You an' de yutha gentleman." She looked at old Pauly.

"An' I'm in charge of the boat."

"Yassa, I expect so."

"And we don't want no nanny goat aroun'. Wasn't supposed to save no goat, nowhow. Goin' to catch hell."

"Yassa."

Ella looked away, moving her lips constantly. Ed
wrinkled his humorous nose and winked to Pauly.

The refugee barge, blacker than the shore, bore sev-

eral tents with torchlight shining through the flaps.
Neighborly aromas floated out to Ella, frying pork and
collards boiling. A rope flung through the dark fell across
the goat. "One female colored!" Ed called.
"Christ! where'll we put her?" cried a doctor who
needed shaving. "Go on, then, report her for inoculation.
All right, open up, folks!"
A group gathered round.
"Where yall from, Cap? Weber's Landin'?"
"Chunky? Dat you Chunky?"
"They got a goat! Look the nanny goat, honey!"
"Make them shut that radio. Woman in labor in that
doctor tent!"
"Denner for whites! Denner for whites! Sengle file,
folks, sengle file!"
Ella did not know anyone. She gave the goat to a boy
and hunted food. Ed had told her to wait for him behind
the white people's bath tent. The crowd did not want her,
nor she the crowd. To her they were like the stars of
heaven for multitude — everybody talking, one big voice,
like the groans of the slain, except some were laughing.
And a preacher somewhere was holding prayer. It was all
magic, sad, wonderful. Ella was sixteen. She had read the
Bible and hoped soon to become an Upper Virgin in the
Watchers of the Double Cave. She studied the calm black
waters. A flood works softly, softly, mantling the
meadows in cool fluid sorrow. Men near by were discuss-
ing the drowned cows and inundated crops. Women
round a charcoal furnace drank coffee, blowing into the
huge tin cups before each sip, anxiously glancing at the
tent where the woman was having the baby. Ella crossed
her hands on her bosom and listened to the unknown
preacher. He was telling his hearers to pray for the white
folks who had saved them alive, or Jesus might still
deliver them up to flood or set them down somewhere in a
plain full of bones.
Ed came with his flashlight. "Ready to go down to the
levee?" One of his hands found the firm bulge of hip

clothed in the new gingham dress.

"Yassa. When you say."

They started for the gangway, but Ed saw some men assembled there.

"Listen, you know how to count?" he asked Ella.

"Yassa."

"I'll go first. When I reach shore you begin countin' slow. When you reach a hundred, come on ashore and go on down the levee. I'll be waitin' in them pin oaks." His hands prowled up and rested in the deep warm hollow between her shoulder blades — trembling. "Look, don't you gyp me, now! You won't gyp me?"

"Nawsa."

"Swear?"

"Yassa."

"What do you swear to, Brown?"

"Jesus."

When Ella had counted past eighty the Coastguard boat came quickly to take the colored people to the receiving station in Baton Rogue. Officials and nurses ran about calling, "Colored over there! All colored!"

Ella hesitated, then hid herself behind the bath tent. A voice behind a blinding flashlight called to her, "Hey! You colored?" She answered, "Yes." "Over this way, an' make it snappy!" But when the light went away she made for the shore gangway. A nurse found her and ordered her to the other side. When the nurse left Ella continued to the shore plank, but there she was brusquely directed to the river side of the barge.

"Cap, I got to go asho'."

"Cain heppit."

Ella crossed the barge and joined the Negroes climbing down. She looked once over her shoulder. Far down the levee Ed was yodeling:

"O de ole lady!
De ole lady who-o-o-o-o!"

The load of negroes went to Baton Rouge and were slept and fed until the water receded. Ella was sick from the serum. She stayed for a day after the others had gone. Then she went to Colonel Jessup's garage. After she had been there several times, peering into the building of oily shadows, a mechanic asked her what she wanted. Ella hurried away but went back round the block and returned. She met the colored porter. He told her Ed Jefferson had quit the Colonel a long time ago. He thought Ed was now with the U-Drive-It.

Ella could not find Ed Jefferson. She returned to Tête Noir. She helped her old mother shovel the mud and leaves through the windows. The mattress was ruined, the chairs warped, the bureau drawers would not come out. With a hatchet they demolished the bureau to get to their clothes.

The Red Cross delivered flour, beans, and coffee, but no dry stovewood could be found. They dug a few sticks from under the soft mud in the yard and put them in the sun.

"Is dis house established an' peaceful?" called the preacher from his mule.

"Yes, Revvin!"

"Praise de livin' Jesus!"

"Yes, Revvin!"

One day Ella's mother said, "Ella chile, take yo' bath soon in the mawnin' and hunt you somethin' to do on the big road. I got sad visions."

Ella, "Yes, mam, I better start for town. A Raid Cross lady to de station promise me a job of work."

"What size job of work?"

"A fried-potato job. Her husband sell fried potatoes. They cooks in de showcase on Reflection Street."

"An' mind out you don't go 'bout no evil in town, bringin' down my gray hairs with sorrow to hell."

Until a late hour every night Ella McCoy worked in the show window on Reflection Street. The potato-chipping machine opened and closed like a polished fist; and next to it an oval vat of golden oil bubbled over blue tongues of gas. There was a salt shaker big enough for a giant, and a stack of waxed bags labeled: HOSTES-SPUDS. The hostesses themselves came in the evening in big cars of all colors, and honked their horns. Ella would run to the curb attired in blue and gray, the company's colors, wearing her silver star between her breasts.

In a month she made enough money to send her mother the cost of new house furnishings and two settings of Minorca eggs. Ella left her job on a rainy day, took a bath, and went round to various garages.

She found Ed next morning early. He was entering the Triangle Better Service Station. Walking fast, he winked at Ella and kept on going into the garage. Suddenly he hastened back to the sidewalk.

"Holy Christ! Say, you look different. Don't you know me?"

"Yassa, Mr. Aid." She allowed herself to be led into the dark building behind a car. "Trying to slip by me, Brown?" the man asked. "You done forget who save your life? Can't you kiss me?"

"Yassa."

"I'm kissin', but you ain't. You want some anti-freeze? How long you be in town? What was your name?"

"Long as you wants, I reckonsa. Ella McCoy."

Ella stayed in Baton Rouge several days longer. Jefferson had a car, or rather a yellow truck chassis with a seat and no body. They would drive down the river road and fool round the woods or levee. Once Ella lost her silver star. She was so concerned that Ed the next day cast her another star from an old main bearing of a caterpillar tractor.

"I better be gettin' home," she said, "if you satisfied."

"I'd like to know who's stoppin' you!" said Ed. "You think I'm crazy about a woman watches the mail plane when she's makin' love?"

Back home in Tête Noir, Ella changed the shelf paper and whitewashed the fence. Each night with her mother she prayed at the fireplace to Jesus who was so kind.

One day the Watchers of the Double Cave gave a sweet-corn boil for the steeple fund. When the people were leaving church, after several reluctant attempts Ella approached the preacher.

"Revvin, pleasa, when can I get to hang my sacred star on the outside my dress?" She wanted to become a Virgin, and also, the babbit metal star had made a sore between her breasts.

The preacher said, "Not untel you becomes a Upper Virgin. You takes dat degree when you reaches seventeen without willin' sin *through* de flesh of thy body. *Now!* Is you seventeen?"

Ella thoughtfully traced semicircles in the dust with her toe.

"Is you seventeen, Ella?"

"Yes, Revvin, Monday was a week."

The preacher pinched her chin. "Well now, you just go in the vestry and ax Sister Orelia instruc' you. De Double Cave convokes a month from today. It'll cost you fo' bits, and you wants to spade you a flower garden fo' de altar right away, an' Jesus bless yo' little soul."

Ella slipped home. In the afternoon on the gallery she stitched thoughtfully at a dress. The Tête Noir people were happier than before the flood — husbands and wives miraculously reunited after a stimulating separation; every able man employed on the new levee; and in the flood-enriched gardens rows of vegetables [flourishing. Of the flood there] remained but a dry brown line drawn at the same height on every wall or tree.

After some days Ella became restless and forced herself to visit Sister Orelia, to learn whether the circumstances of her transgression were excusable enough to permit of her becoming an Upper Virgin. The old crone with her pipe was sorry, but nothing could be done. However, if she wished, Ella might be admitted to the Cave as a Lower Virgin. If she decided to do that, Ella must be sponsored by a guardian angel, a girl under seventeen whose heart was free from willing sin. If and when the guardian angel attained seventeen without sin, then both would be admissible as Upper Virgins.

Ella decided to forget about the Double Cave. Her life, however, became pretty blue and empty. In the night she sat on the gallery until the roosters crowed in the fog. So she began to think of a possible sponsor. Among the Tête Noir girls was one named Gladys, of fourteen years, who was known to be free from willing sin. Ella did not care much for Gladys. She went to see her. Ella worked around slantways to the topic of the Double Cave.

"I'm goin' in de Cave nex' month," Gladys said, "guarding angel fo' my second cousin. Six people wants me to sponsor them. This place done run out of sponsors is de trouble."

Ella returned to her gallery and folded her hands.

About this time some new people moved next door to Ella, city people, a man, woman, and child. The man, called Flip, was a chauffeur for a levee engineer. He was big and sophisticated and tough, of the peculiar dark oily color known as crankcase brown. Flip and his woman were always quarreling violently. It seemed a certain man, former admirer of the wife, had followed them to Tête Noir. Ella saw Flip stand for hours at the corner, watching his house with his long legs crossed in the shape of a figure four.

The child, six years old, was named Rancie. She was afraid of nothing but her father. Even then when Flip came home to beat his wife's head, Rancie, hiding in the blackberry bushes, would throw handfuls of green berries toward the house and whisper in a voice deep as a man's, "Big ugly mule-bear! Big mule-bear you!" She was skinny, black as treachery, and wore only a pair of gray drawers. Her chest was sunken and her feet huge, incredibly thick, as if the flesh of her legs had softened and run down there. She kept her bits of colored glass and other playthings in the blackberry bushes; and from the window Ella saw Rancie crawl from the bushes without sign of a thorn scratch and wondered what kind of skin Rancie had. Ella was a long time coaxing Rancie to be friends, because the child was wild and shy. Ella prayed for Rancie and gave her table scraps; and for a time was able to forget about the Double Cave.

Flip kept his wife's street clothes locked up; but one day the woman picked the lock. She went out somewhere, and shortly after her return Flip drove up in his boss's car, came in, and found his woman all dressed up.

Flip spread his legs in the doorway, making a long triangular shadow on the floor in the setting sun. He put his thumb in his belt and began to grin, not a bit surprised. Then he took out his thirty-eight and said, "Stop me ef you done heard this story befo'," and shot the woman in the face.

Ella, next door, yelled and jumped the fence that she had never before been able to climb and ran for the blackberry bushes. Rancie was just crawling out, all bleeding from thorn scratches.

"Quick, Sugar!" whispered Ella. "Jesus heppus!" And she took Rancie home.

The night after Ella went to court she and Rancie sat hand in hand on Ella's gallery.

"Who was it save yo' life yonder?" Ella asked.

"*You* save my life!"

"You goin' to treat me white, Sugar?"

"Yassam."

"You goin' to be my little guarding angel and march aside of me in the nice procession, and live wid me untel I'm old and full of days?"

"Yas, *mam,* Miss Ella!"

But Ella did not know how to break the news to her mother.

Next morning at breakfast table she said to Rancie, "Rancie, Sugar, tell yo' new grammaw what you wants to do for Ella savin' yo' life yonder."

"I wants to be a little guarding angel in de procession."

"What's all dis?" asked the old woman.

"I'm goin' in de Double Cave somehow."

"But you's a Upper Virgin, Ella!"

"Nome. Lower."

Ella dipped the cornbread into her bowl of molasses.
The older woman went slowly round the table and took
Ella's cornbread and syrup away from her and carried it
out back to the hog. Ella got up and began to gather her
belongings. The mother remained in the back yard until
she heard the front door slam softly.

Ella and Rancie stayed in the woods one night, but the
next morning they found an abandoned shack on the
front of town, high up where the water would never rise.
They managed to get the furniture from Flip's house,
which nobody wanted, and Ella cut scalloped shelf paper
from rotogravure sections and whitewashed the fence.
She at once spaded up her flower garden for the altar and
found washing to do for white people, a bundle each day.

Ella got in the Double Cave on a pretty Sunday morning when the grass was all wet and the tulip trees in
bloom. In the class were ten other Virgins, all Lower
ones. The procession trudged the snaky dirt road, and at
the cemetery prayers were said over the graves of two or
three departed Virgins. Returning to church, they
marched past the homes of the three Chief Upper
Matrons, each of whom was clad in white robes and
golden stars, waiting to come outside and give out a
blessing. The last of the matrons visited was Ella's
mother.

The preacher gave the Five Knocks and went in to
fetch her. She covered her face and came out calling the
ritual greeting, "Who pilgrims this house *on* the Lord's
morning?"

The Virgins chanted together, "Eleven Virgins pure,
and crave your deep blessing, dear Matron!"

Ella's mother was looking fixedly at Ella, whose head-
dress was put on improperly, needing adjustment. The
preacher began prompting the Matron in a croaking
whisper, "My blessing — "

"My blessing I freely give! Go forth and tend the bud of

renown. An' mind out yo' veils is straight on yo' stubborn haid."

So Ella at last became a Virgin, one of the hardest things to do. Thenceforth she worked hard and minded her own business and took good care of her little guardian angel. The two lived in peace, bothered by no one, and the garden bore flowers of four colors, and the hens grew tame, coming up to pick at Ella's shoe. Her burden grew small and vanished, gentler than the wind takes a patch of snow.

Not even Ed Jefferson disturbed them very much when he came one fall day looking for Ella.

When she saw the yellow truck with a seat and no body, Ella called Rancie from the kitchen. Rancie had a stick of sugar cane in her hand.

"I was passing by here," Jefferson explained. "Been huntin' you all over town, includin' the graveyard. The sexton sent me to the preacher and the preacher sent me here. You know all the big shots. Say, ain't you all got no lunchroom in this town?"

Ella brought up a chair. "Rancie, get the gentleman a glass of cow's milk and some veal meat," she said.

Ed tackled the lunch. "Your meat is tender but your knife is tough," he said. Rancie stood in a dim corner, looking at the stranger with her big eyes shining, her finger in her mouth, and holding the sugar cane. The hens out back sang busily.

"Well, I done quit the Triangle," said Ed, wiping his mouth.

Ella smiled politely and smoothed down her braided hair. Silence fell.

"I'm chauffeur for a rich white man now," said Ed.

Ella looked through the window. Rancie kept watching the man. Ed glanced at her, coughed, wiped his brow. "Nice little place you all got." He glanced at Rancie, with Ella's leaden star on her bosom. Ed reached into his pocket. "Here's you a nickel, Sis," he told Rancie. "Don't you want to go eat your cane down by the river? You got a knife? Brown, I could spend a Sunday here sharpenin' knives alone."

Rancie placed the nickel in her ear. She did not move or blink. Her huge splayed feet seemed to grip the floor tightly. Ed's eyes traveled up and down the stick of cane. He shrugged and spat in the fireplace.

Ed sauntered over to peer into the kitchen, then crossed to Ella. "When you comin' back to town, Brown?" He put his hand on the chair back. "Huh?" His hand wandered and rested on Ella's shoulder skin, where there was only a thin cotton strap.

Then abruptly Rancie marched over and stood beside Ella with the stalk of cane, which was twice as tall as she. She took Ella's hand and fixed her big white eyes upon the stranger.

Ed glared at the guardian angel for a long time, while no sound was heard but the contended singing of hens. Then Ed jerked up his belt and strolled uncertainly toward the door, lingering at the mantelpiece to glance at a Kodak picture of the procession. "Nice place you all got. I thought I'd say hello. You look me up when you come to town." On the porch he said, "So long, Brown. It looks like rain."

"Good-bye, Mr. Aid," Ella called, "and thanksa for comin' aroun'."

Rancie sank to the floor and chewed on the sugar cane, tearing off long purple strips of skin. Her teeth were very strong.

The Little Convent Girl

GRACE KING

She was coming down on the boat from Cincinnati, the little convent girl. Two sisters had brought her aboard. They gave her in charge of the captain, got her a state-room, saw that the new little trunk was put into it, hung the new little satchel up on the wall, showed her how to bolt the door at night, shook hands with her for good-by (good-bys have really no significance for sisters), and left her there. After a while the bells all rang, and the boat, in the awkward elephantine fashion of boats, got into midstream. The chambermaid found her sitting on the chair in the state-room where the sisters had left her, and showed her how to sit on a chair in the saloon. And there she sat until the captain came and hunted her up for supper. She could not do anything of herself; she had to be initiated into everything by some one else.

She was known on the boat only as "the little convent girl." Her name, of course, was registered in the clerk's office, but on a steamboat no one thinks of consulting the clerk's ledger. It is always the little widow, the fat madam, the tall colonel, the parson, etc. The captain, who pronounced by the letter, always called her the little convent girl. She was the beau-ideal of the little convent girl. She never raised her eyes except when spoken to. Of course she never spoke first, even to the chambermaid, and when she did speak it was in the wee, shy, furtive voice one might imagine a just-budding violet to have; and she walked with such soft, easy, carefully calculated steps that one naturally felt the penalties that must have secured them — penalties dictated by a black code of deportment.

She was dressed in deep mourning. Her black straw hat was trimmed with stiff new crape, and her stiff new bombazine dress had crape collar and cuffs. She wore her hair in two long plaits fastened around her head tight and fast. Her hair had a strong inclination to curl, but that had been taken out of it as austerely as the noise out of her footfalls. Her hair was as black as her dress; her eyes, when one saw them, seemed blacker than either, on account of the bluishness of the white surrounding the pupil. Her eyelashes were almost as thick as the black veil which the sisters had fastened around her hat with an extra pin the very last thing before leaving. She had a round little face, and a tiny pointed chin; her mouth was slightly protuberant from the teeth, over which she tried to keep her lips well shut, the effort giving them a pathetic little forced expression. Her complexion was sallow, a pale sallow, the complexion of a brunette bleached in darkened rooms. The only color about her was a blue taffeta ribbon from which a large silver medal of the Virgin hung over the place where a breastpin should have been. She was so little, so little, although she was eighteen, as the sisters told the captain; otherwise they would not have permitted her to travel all the way to New Orleans alone.

Unless the captain or the clerk remembered to fetch her out in front, she would sit all day in the cabin, in the

KING

same place, crocheting lace, her spool of thread and box of patterns in her lap, on the handkerchief spread to save her new dress. Never leaning back — oh, no! always straight and stiff, as if the conventual back board were there within call. She would eat only convent fare at first, notwithstanding the importunities of the waiters, and the jocularities of the captain, and particularly of the clerk. Every one knows the fund of humor possessed by a steamboat clerk, and what a field for display the table at meal-times affords. On Friday she fasted rigidly, and she never began to eat, or finished, without a little Latin movement of the lips and a sign of the cross. And always at six o'clock of the evening she remembered the angelus, although there was no church bell to remind her of it.

She was in mourning for her father, the sisters told the captain, and she was going to New Orleans to her mother. She had not seen her mother since she was an infant, on account of some disagreement between the parents, in consequence of which the father had brought her to Cincinnati, and placed her in the convent. There she had been for twelve years, only going to her father for vacations and holidays. So long as the father lived he would never let the child have any communication with her mother. Now that he was dead all that was changed, and the first thing that the girl herself wanted to do was to go to her mother.

The mother superior had arranged it all with the mother of the girl, who was to come personally to the boat in New Orleans and receive her child from the captain, presenting a letter from the mother superior, a facsimile of which the sisters gave the captain.

It is a long voyage from Cincinnati to New Orleans, the rivers doing their best to make it interminable, embroidering themselves *ad libitum* all over the country. Every five miles, and sometimes oftener, the boat would stop to put off or take on freight, if not both. The little convent girl, sitting in the cabin, had her terrible frights at first from the hideous noises attendant on these land-

180

ings — the whistles, the ringings of the bells, the running to and fro, the shouting. Every time she thought it was shipwreck, death, judgment, purgatory; and her sins! her sins! She would drop her crochet, and clutch her prayer-beads from her pocket, and relax the constraint over her lips, which would go to rattling off prayers with the velocity of a relaxed windlass. That was at first, before the captain took to fetching her out in front to see the boat make a landing. Then she got to liking it so much that she would stay all day just where the captain put her, going inside only for her meals. She forgot herself at times so much that she would draw her chair a little closer to the railing, and put up her veil, actually, to see better. No one ever usurped her place, quite in front, or intruded upon her either with word or look; for every one learned to know her shyness, and began to feel a personal interest in her, and all wanted the little convent girl to see everything that she possibly could.

And it was worth seeing — the balancing and *chasséing* and waltzing of the cumbersome old boat to make a landing. It seemed to be always attended with the difficulty and the improbability of a new enterprise; and the relief when it did sidle up anywhere within rope's-throw of the spot aimed at! And the roustabout throwing the rope from the perilous end of the dangling gang-plank! And the dangling roustabouts hanging like drops of water from it — dropping sometimes twenty feet to the land, and not infrequently into the river itself. And then what a rolling of barrels, and shouldering of sacks, and singing of Jim Crow songs, and pacing of Jim Crow steps; and black skins glistening through torn shirts, and white teeth gleaming through red lips, and laughing, and talking and — bewildering! entrancing! Surely the little convent girl in her convent walls never dreamed of so much unpunished noise and movement in the world!

The first time she heard the mate — it must have been like the first time woman ever heard man — curse and swear, she turned pale, and ran quickly, quickly into the

181

saloon, and — came out again? No, indeed! not with all the soul she had to save, and all the other sins on her conscience. She shook her head resolutely, and was not seen in her chair on deck again until the captain not only reassured her, but guaranteed his reassurance. And after that, whenever the boat was about to make a landing, the mate would first glance up to the guards, and if the little convent girl was sitting there he would change his invective to sarcasm, and politely request the colored gentlemen not to hurry themselves — on no account whatever; to take their time about shoving out the plank; to send the rope ashore by post-office — write him when it got there; begging them not to strain their backs; calling them mister, colonel, major general, prince, and your royal highness, which was vastly amusing. At night, however, or when the little convent girl was not there, language flowed in its natural curve, the mate swearing like a pagan to make up for lost time.

The captain forgot himself one day: it was when the boat ran aground in the most unexpected manner and place, and he went to work to express his opinion, as only steamboat captains can, of the pilot, mate, engineer, crew, boat, river, country, and the world in general, ringing the bell, first to back, then to head, shouting himself hoarser than his own whistle — when he chanced to see the little black figure hurrying through the chaos on the deck; and the captain stuck as fast aground in midstream as the boat had done.

In the evening the little convent girl would be taken on the upper deck, and going up the steep stairs there was such confusion, to keep the black skirts well over the stiff white petticoats; and, coming down, such blushing when suspicion would cross the unprepared face that a rim of white stocking might be visible; and the thin feet, laced so tightly in the glossy new leather boots, would cling to each successive step as if they could never, never make another venture; and then one boot would (there is but that word) hesitate out, and feel and feel around, and have such a pause of helpless agony as if indeed the next step must have been wilfully removed, or was nowhere to be found on the wide, wide earth.

It was a miracle that the pilot ever got her up into the pilot-house; but pilots have a lonely time, and do not hesitate even at miracles when there is a chance for company. He would place a box for her to climb to the tall bench behind the wheel, and he would arrange the cushions, and open a window here to let in air, and shut one there to cut off a draft, as if there could be no tenderer consideration in life for him than her comfort. And he would talk of the river to her, explain the chart, pointing out eddies, whirlpools, shoals, depths, new beds, old beds, cut-offs, caving banks, and making banks, as exquisitely and respectfully as if she had been the River Commission.

It was his opinion that there was as great a river as the Mississippi flowing directly under it — an underself of a river, as much a counterpart of the other as the second story of a house is of the first; in fact, he said they were navigating through the upper story. Whirlpools were holes in the floor of the upper river, so to speak; eddies were rifts and cracks. And deep under the earth, hurrying toward the subterranean stream, were other streams, small and great, but all deep, hurrying to and from that great mother-stream underneath, just as the small and great overground streams hurry to and from their mother Mississippi. It was almost more than the little convent girl could take in: at least such was the expression of her eyes; for they opened as all eyes have to open at pilot stories. And he knew as much of astronomy as he did of hydrology, could call the stars by name, and define the shapes of the constellations; and she, who had studied astronomy at the convent, was charmed to find that what she had learned was all true. It was in the pilot-house, one night, that she forgot herself for the first time in her life, and stayed up until after nine o'clock. Although she appeared almost intoxicated at the wild pleasure, she was immediately overwhelmed at the wickedness of it, and observed much more rigidity of conduct thereafter. The engineer, the boiler-men, the firemen, the stokers, they all knew when the little convent girl was up in the pilot-house: the speaking-tube became so mild and gentle.

With all the delays of river and boat, however, there is an end of the journey from Cincinnati to New Orleans. The latter city, which at one time to the impatient seemed at the terminus of the never, began, all of a sudden, one day to make its nearingness felt; and from that period every other interest paled before the interest in the immanence of arrival into port, and the whole boat was seized with a panic of preparation, the little convent girl with the others. Although so immaculate was she in person and effects that she might have been struck with a landing, as some good people might be struck with death, at any moment without fear of results, her trunk was packed and repacked, her satchel arranged and rearranged, and, the last day, her hair was brushed and plaited and smoothed over and over again until the very last glimmer of a curl disappeared. Her dress was whisked, as if for microscopic inspection; her face was washed; and her finger-nails were scrubbed with the hard convent nail-brush, until the disciplined little tips ached with a pristine soreness. And still there were hours to wait, and still the boat added up delays. But she arrived at last, after all, with not more than the usual and expected difference between the actual and the advertised time of arrival.

There was extra blowing and extra ringing, shouting, commanding, rushing up the gangway and rushing down the gangway. The clerks, sitting behind tables on the first deck, were plied, in the twinkling of an eye, with estimates, receipts, charges, countercharges, claims, reclaims, demands, questions, accusations, threats, all at topmost voices. None but steamboat clerks could have stood it. And there were throngs composed of individuals every one of whom wanted to see the captain first and at once: and those who could not get to him shouted over the heads of the others; and as usual he lost his temper and politeness, and began to do what he termed "hustle."

"Captain! Captain!" a voice called him to where a hand plucked his sleeve, and a letter was thrust toward him. "The cross, and the name of the convent." He recognized the envelop of the mother superior. He read the duplicate of the letter given by the sisters. He looked at the woman — the mother — casually, then again and again.

The little convent girl saw him coming, leading some one toward her. She rose. The captain took her hand first, before the other greeting. "Good-by, my dear," he said. He tried to add something else, but seemed undetermined what. "Be a good little girl — " It was evidently all he could think of. Nodding to the woman behind him, he turned on his heel, and left.

One of the deck-hands was sent to fetch her trunk. He walked out behind them, through the cabin, and the crowd on deck, down the stairs, and out over the gangway. The little convent girl and her mother went with hands tightly clasped. She did not turn her eyes to the right or left, or once (what all passengers do) look backward at the boat which, however slowly, had carried her surely over dangers that she wot not of. All looked at her as she passed. All wanted to say good-by to the little convent girl, to see the mother who had been deprived of her so long. Some expressed surprise in a whistle; some in other ways. All exclaimed audibly, or to themselves, "Colored!"

It takes about a month to make the round trip from New Orleans to Cincinnati and back, counting five days' stoppage in New Orleans. It was a month to a day when the steamboat came puffing and blowing up to the wharf again, like a stout dowager after too long a walk; and the same scene of confusion was enacted, as it had been enacted twelve times a year, at almost the same wharf for twenty years; and the same calm, a death calmness by contrast, followed as usual the next morning.

The decks were quiet and clean; one cargo had just been delivered, part of another stood ready on the levee to be shipped. The captain was there waiting for his business to begin, the clerk was in his office getting his books ready, the voice of the mate could be heard below, mustering the old crew out and a new crew in; for if steamboat crews have a single principle, — and there are those who deny them any, — it is never to ship twice in succession on the same boat. It was too early yet for any but roustabouts, marketers, and church-goers; so early that even the river was still partly mist-covered; only in places could the swift, dark current be seen rolling swiftly along.

"Captain!" A hand plucked at his elbow, as if not confident that the mere calling would secure attention. The captain turned. The mother of the little convent girl stood there, and she held the little convent girl by the hand. "I have brought her to see you," the woman said. "You were so kind — and she is so quiet, so still, all the time, I thought it would do her a pleasure."

She spoke with an accent, and with embarrassment; otherwise one would have said that she was bold and assured enough.

"She don't go nowhere, she don't do nothing but make her crochet and her prayers, so I thought I would bring her for a little visit of 'How d'ye do' to you."

There was, perhaps, some inflection in the woman's voice that might have made known, or at least awakened, the suspicion of some latent hope or intention, had the captain's ear been fine enough to detect it. There might have been something in the little convent girl's face, had his eye been more sensitive — a trifle paler, maybe, the lips a little tighter drawn, the blue ribbon a shade faded. He may have noticed that, but — And the visit of "How d'ye do" came to an end.

They walked down the stairway, the woman in front, the little convent girl — her hand released to shake hands with the captain — following, across the bared deck, out to the gangway, over to the middle of it. No one was looking, no one saw more than a flutter of white petticoats, a show of white stockings, as the little convent girl went under the water.

The roustabout dived, as the roustabouts always do, after the drowning, even at the risk of their good-for-nothing lives. The mate himself jumped overboard; but she had gone down in a whirlpool. Perhaps, as the pilot had told her whirlpools always did, it may have carried her through to the underground river, to that vast, hidden, dark Mississippi that flows beneath the one we see; for her body was never found.

Daughter of Lescale

E. EARL SPARLING

René Lescale came in from the wharves later than was
his wont, for he had been on the job alone. Burt, his
helper, was laid up with dengue fever.

The old Frenchman was tired, hungry, cold. A pene-
trating fog had come up the River, despite the wet wind
blowing from the far side. The fog and the wind bit into
him. He always wore only his thin, short coat under the
wharves. That left his legs unhampered. There was
never any telling when the whistles might shriek and the
lights blaze up and safety would depend on free arms
and legs.

He took a last look at the River as he breasted the top of
the levee between two hulking warehouses, and
shrugged by way of thanking Providence that at least
one more night was passed without untoward events.
Then, taking only time to stow his loot in the usual place,
he shuffled hurriedly out old Hospital Street which leads
into Bayou Road.

In spite of the fog that was momentarily closing about him and turning the street into a dank, cheerless canyon with formidable walls and threatening cliffs of galleries — despite it René Lescale hummed to himself. He was thinking not of the fog and the street lamps that tried dismally to stab through it at every corner, but of his little home in Elysian Fields. Elise, his daughter, would be waiting for him with a big pot of coffee dripped and ready for the cup. And when Elise made coffee she made it — black as ink, smooth as satin, and strong as the devil.

Always Elise sat up waiting for him and that did his heart good. Ever since the old mother had died, Elise had taken charge of this household, and, truth being told, she managed it with a better hand. She imparted cheer and bravery to it. She always laughed when the old mother would probably have wept a bit.

No matter what hour old dad came in from the River his daughter was waiting for him. Sometimes she dozed on the leather duo-fold in the front room of the squat little house, but never did it take more than his step on the stoop to awaken her. And knowing that she would be waiting served to bring him in sooner than he would have come otherwise. That lessened the danger that hung over him of nights by just that much.

Elise had tried on occasions to get him to give up his work. She had tried both argument and tears. Old dad would listen to anything else she advised, but to such things he turned a deaf ear.

"But no," he always answered. "For ten years I have done this, me, and there was no danger. It does not billong that I quit yet. Som'day when I hav' so many dollaire we hav' whatsoeveh we want I leave this bizness."

He would pat her fondly on the head and that would end it. It did not end it in the heart of the girl, however. From the age of twelve, when she first discovered how he made his living, she had realized the danger, the danger that ever hangs upon the footsteps of those who laugh at the law and its majesty. Now at the age of seventeen she realized it more than ever. And each night as she waited for his return she was tense, and never did she really relax until she heard his shuffling step.

So, knowing these things, René Lescale hummed as he moved through the fog, for it was good for a man getting along in his years to have such a daughter, strong and young and lovely, waiting for him. The old Frenchman walked faster as he neared his home. But as he came in sight of it he became conscious that something was wrong.

There was no light in the front room glimmering out merrily to greet him. At first he thought it was the fog, that the light could not pierce through the condensing vapors. But as he got still nearer he saw that truly for the first time there was no light.

As he hastened up the stoop, now in a real hurry, it was not thrown open. No strong, young shape was framed in the entrance. No cheerful voice welcomed him. The house was cold and dark as he flung the door open himself.

"Eh . . . Elise . . . Elise."

His voice echoed vacantly. No answer came to him, and he fumbled for the light, suddenly fearing.

"Elise . . . where h-are you, my child, Elise."

He became frantic and went rushing through the house, calling ever more loudly, colliding against the furniture, turning the orderly rooms into a confusion. He searched every room twice — in vain.

Then he found the note lying casually on the kitchen table beside the cold coffee pot. It was scribbled on the back of an old envelope. It was brief. Elise had gone away with Burt O'Reilly because she loved that Irish lad. Old dad must not be sad nor angry.

Lescale sat staring at it, reading it over once and again. Then he buried his face in his hands, the veins in his arms growing knotted. Finally he raised his arms to the corners of the room and spoke of vengeance.

"Not for nothing can this be made by me. Som'day he shall pay. He shall make for it in a way *terrible*. No one breaks up my 'ouse. I take him like my h-own. I teach him. I make for him money. And with this he thanks me back. He shall r-r-regret this night."

Then he got away from his English and spoke brutally in French.

There was a fairness in much that he said, for he had made the blunt Irish boy, Burt O'Reilly, everything that he was. He had taught him things that at least no man ever learned in books.

The old man had found the boy up in the Irish Channel, pursuing a paltry profession, robbing slot machines and butchers' cash drawers, lounging with corner gangs betimes, taking life as he found it and making nothing of it. Lescale saw in him certain chance possibilities and took an interest in him. He took him down into the Quarter and there taught him things as he knew them. He taught him his own business as he had developed it by years of hard application.

With his gray straightforward eyes and his lively brain, the boy was an apt apprentice. He took to the wharves almost as smoothly as the brown turmoil of water that swept ever by and past them. And so, René Lescale, aging Frenchman, and Burt O'Reilly, young Irishman, became business partners. And a good business it was for any who could look a little chance danger in the face. There was no overhead; there was fast turn-over with high profit.

Any favorably dark night you could find them slinking along Water Road or Delta Street — that is, of course, if you knew where to look. And it would never have done to ask of the wharf watchman, for the watchmen were the last ones to know. It was only in the morning that the watchmen knew where they had been, and then it was much too late for anyone to find them.

Or, if you did not find them slinking along the roads that skirt the waterfront, you might find them going cat-like down under the black pilings of the wharves, their feet picking slippery holds here and there and mostly nowhere, their voices muffled by the slappings and lappings of the waters close under them. You *might* find them thus. On the other hand, if you went under the wharves seeking them you would probably end dismally in the black shifting waters that boil, eddy, and slap with an oily undertow. Only after long practice does any man go under the wharves at night.

Wharf rats the two were called in the parlance of the waterfront, and though that profession is not as honored as some, they at least met its exigencies with care and exactitude. The Frenchman had the necessary cunning. The young Irishman had the stamina and the daring. An old head and a young heart make a formidable pair under any circumstances.

No expensive and elaborate equipment did these business men of the wharves need. A sharpened *machette,* relic of some sugar plantation, and a close-meshed gunny sack; that was all. No brace of yeggs were ever armed more casually.

Down under the wharves they would slither until they came beneath a freshly arrived shipment of produce, the position of which had been well remarked beforetime. Coffee, Mexican beans, rice, sugar — it was all the same to them if it were salable loot. Up through the cracks in the wharf flooring would go the knife to find profitable resting place. As the plunder trickled down from the ripped sacks it was caught in their own sack and the night's work was done. Seldom did they come up from the wharves without at least one well-filled sack.

It was profitable business even in the old days. After prohibition came it boomed, for the firm of Lescale and O'Reilly found it just as easy to rifle an alcohol drum as a coffee sack. A steel drill was merely substituted for the *machette.*

The alcohol came from the industrial plants. It was shipped through the wharves to outbound boats. One pint of alcohol was more valuable than an entire sack of coffee, for those of the Quarter did not understand this new law which would take the zest out of living. They would have their whisky, cognac, absinthe. More than one bottle of the bonded goods that went over the counters was manufactured from the alcohol brought up industriously by Lescale and O'Reilly.

The two waxed prosperous, and their days were filled with plenty, and the old Frenchman began to look forward to the time when he really could give up his business with content. But . . .

Well, a young heart does other things than add stamina and daring to undertakings. Burt O'Reilly fell in love with Elise, daughter of René Lescale. From the first day he saw the girl he knew in his own Irish way that he must have her. Her quiet beauty had a quenching effect upon him. There was something in her manner so unlike the things the boy had found in women he had known that it placed her apart to be worshipped and desired. Burt O'Reilly, being Irish, went straight to the old Frenchman.

"I'm after marrying your girl," he said, just so abruptly.

René Lescale looked at him as though he did not quite believe what he was hearing.

"W'at it is you say?"

"I say," repeated the boy, "I want to marry Elise."

"Hah. You come at me to marrie *ma fille*, my h-own. You h-are one fool."

"Now lissen . . ."

"You lissen, maybe. W'at you h-are to think like such a one fool. You h-are nothing. You h-are the strit. You h-are the gutter. You think like this, then no more I want to fin' you by me daughter, no."

Much more René Lescale told the boy and it left him wilted in spirit, but it did not take away his love. And so, he took Elise in the best way he knew to do so, and left affairs to straighten themselves.

Now if the love of the Irish lad were blunt, the cunning

193

of the Frenchman was acute. Did old René Lescale go forth and up and down to find Burt and vent his vengeance upon him? Did he move swiftly, directly? He did not. Carefully, skilfully, he let it be known that he bore the lad no ill will. He choked down the things that sprang to his tongue, and planted a smile on his lips, an indulgent, paternal smile.

"I was young yet, meself," he said. "Hah. Love is w'at you never know what it will do. Me hav' the anger. Ah no. Why should that, eh?"

He dropped such words in places where he well calculated they would find their way to his daughter and the blackguard who had stolen her. And fate worked with a steady hand. When the word came to Burt that his father-in-law was after all willing to look at things with a reasonable mind he was in need of money. It took money to start housekeeping, even in Irish Channel. When the comfortable word had come two or three times from as several sources he took counsel with himself and his wife.

"I dunno. I dunno," said the boy.

"Oh, he understands," argued the girl. "He loves me. It is all right."

"But he don't love me none after this."

"Such foolishness you talk. He will love you." She wrapped her arms about his neck. "I love you so much that everyone must love you."

Burt had his doubts as to that, but as he observed, "We gotta have coin. That's plain as the wart on the pawnbroker's nose. And I guess I can get it from the old boy quicker than any place else."

Therewith he donned his bravery, and as René Lescale stood up that night to the Yellow Stripe bar there fell a hand on his shoulder. The others around the bar let their glasses down suddenly. Even the boys fresh from the boats sensed something was up. José, behind the bar, laid aside his towel and tightened for trouble.

"Got nerve, that kid," croaked Ratty Pete, who had just

been talking to José. "Got nerve."

But old Lescale fooled them. He played his game. For a long moment he stood looking at the boy. Then he laughed. He laughed and clapped his two hands on the boy's shoulders.

"*Mais* no. It is old Burt, my h-own Burt. *C'est bien.* One more glass again there, my friend. A glass for Burt." Just like that it was. No stir. No rumpus. The old fellow was as smooth about it as though Burt O'Reilly had come back from a mere holiday. Later, after the glasses had passed over the bar several times, Lescale drew the boy aside.

"You mus' know, eh? There is tonight a job. You com' just correct."

"A job. Then yer gonna take me back?"

"*Eh, oui,* me son. We do much job together yet, is it not?"

The boy blurted, but Lescale stopped him.

"That never minds. It is bizness we talk jus' now. The alcohol shipment arrive this ver' day. We do him tonight, w'at you think?"

What was there for Burt O'Reilly to say? There was no getting around a father-in-law like that. Burt just pressed the old fellow's hands and swallowed hard.

As the moon was settling down under the slate roof tops some three hours later, they slipped out from below the old Picayune pier in a little skiff that reeked of soft tar mixed with oil, and headed down the River. Lescale handled the oars. The boy sat in the stern holding the shrouded lantern.

The River's night life had quieted. The noisy tugs were leashed. Only the slow ferries were limping across from one bank to another. Sometimes a far-away whistle bayed mournfully. Lights were doused. From one low-lying Spanish freighter as they passed under its wallowing shadows came the wail of a Seville song, and they caught the plaintive sound of some stringed instrument. From a British boat further downstream came the ribald words of a drunken cockney seaman arguing with the mate on deck watch.

Then they were out of earshot of the comedy, and there was only the creak of the oars in the locks, and the short grunt of the old man as he kept swinging the skiff out of the stiff eddies that hung into the shore. The two were silent for the most part, but after they had gone so far without a stop O'Reilly grew a little doubtful.

"How far yeh going?"

"Below the government dock," grunted Lescale.

"I ain't never heard of them putting alcohol down there."

"They begin to feel careless," explained Lescale. "They think they put him anywhere. They shall learn, eh?"

The boy kept silent again until after they had rounded the government wharves. Then he had to speak the things that were on his mind.

"Yer being might square with me, Ren, after what I done yeh."

The old man did not answer, but his oars missed the water and slapped noisily.

"Yeh know how them things are," the boy went on. "I don't know yet just why I done it. I been feeling about it ever since."

Lescale spoke abruptly. "It is well we do not talk of that things."

"But I been . . . I gotta . . ."

"We shall not speak of those."

Lescale's voice was like a knife. The boy floundered into silence. A moment later the man turned the boat into the shore.

"It is here . . . make quiet."

Lescale tied the boat deftly and stepped into the maze of black, treacherous pilings, leading the way.

"Keep those light covered."

Burt had trouble making his way. He had never been below these wharves before. They were built with more numerous braces and water-line stays than those higher up the river. He stumbled over a cement post and swore silently. He wondered at the older man's agility.

Ahead Lescale gave a low cry, and when the boy came up with him, he pointed above. Burt cautiously raised the lantern cover and ran a short beam along the flooring overhead. The light caught on the iron drums through the cracks.

"Easy," he whispered.

Lescale produced the steel augur. "You go up," he ordered. "I get old for this climbing."

"Correct," agreed the boy, and shedding his coat was in another moment seven feet above with his head close under the flooring.

"The lantern," whispered Lescale, reaching it up to him. "You were better take her. I go to get the cask."

Burt heard him move away toward the boat as he pushed the augur through the widest opening in the flooring. After several false starts he got a good purchase on the iron, settled into position, and began to drill. The oiled steel bit into the iron with a soft purr. It was hard work, but Burt this night hardly noticed it. His heart sang to the purr of the drill. It had all been so much easier than he had expected. Ren was a good old guy — a good old guy.

The boy stopped abruptly to listen. He thought he had heard something, the splash of oars. Only the lapping of the River came to him in the silence, and he grinned sheepishly at his brief suspicion. He applied himself again to the job in hand.

The alcohol drums were always thin. This one seemed even thinner than usual. It was only a matter of moments until he felt the drill pressing. He pushed harder. It went through with a dull, grating sound. The boy gave a low whistle to let Lescale know he was ready for the cask.

But Lescale did not answer, and of a sudden Burt's nose caught a pungent odor.

He sniffed. Cold suspicion flashed on him. He shifted

197

sharply. The bit slipped from his hand. A thin trickle came through the flooring. It fell upon his face and clothing and on the lantern cover. The pungent odor was all about him.

"Gaw . . . gasoline," he gasped.

Fear swept him. He swung for the lantern, lost his balance, and could not stop. He fell across a boarding three feet below.

A great roaring filled his ears, and the night belched into flame about him. All his body was on fire and there was a maelstrom of fire surrounding him.

Far out in the middle of the River René Lescale paused on his oars as the blast lit the sky. And he was pleased.

One of the fabulous million-words-a-year writers, **H. BEDFORD-JONES** was a mighty mainstay of the pulps and one of the few men to make more than a million dollars from his writing alone. Born in Canada in 1897, he spent most of his life in the United States and became a naturalized citizen. Outside of a spell as foreign correspondent of the *Boston Globe,* he was a writer all his life. He wrote every imaginable kind of story well: air-war, mystery, western; but his forte was the historical adventure. "If there was any time in history," said magazine historian Ron Goulart, "when more than two people got into a fight, Bedford-Jones could . . . tell you the exact weapons used." His first book was *The Cross and the Hammer* (1912), a novel of the Crusades; others were *Rhodomont* (1925) and *Cyrano* (1930). Often spiced with a touch of the supernatural, his stories frequently featured such figures as d'Artagnan, Cleopatra, and Cyrano de Bergerac. The editors of *Blue Book* estimated that in 30 years he contributed to it alone 7 serials, 6 book-length novels, and more than 360 short stories and novelettes, often in series such as "Arms and Men," and "The World Was Their Stage." Bedford-Jones died in 1949.

"I was born on the Mississippi River," **ELLIS PARKER BUTLER** reported, in Iowa in 1869. The family was both large and poor, which led to Butler's being mostly reared by his Aunt Lizzie, "a cultured lady who gave me a liking for literature" as well as much of his early education. Leaving high school after a year to work for a grocery, Butler began sending humor and verse to publishers, getting an editorial job in New York in 1897. His second book, *Pigs Is Pigs* (1905), about a small-town postman's hunt for the addressee of a crate of guinea pigs whose population is growing hourly, was a smash success that gave him a lifetime audience for his humorous work — including his creation of one of the best humorous detectives, *Philo Gubb, Correspondence-School Detective (1918).* After a second career in banking and politics, Butler died in 1937.

ERSKINE CALDWELL, one of the most widely read writers in the United States, was born in Georgia in 1903. Due to his father's job as Presbyterian home mission secretary, the family moved so often Caldwell got little formal education early on; later, a year of high school and two years of Gulf Coast travel were followed by a year at the University of Virginia, where he began writing, and three years at the University of Pennsylvania. After seven years of odd jobs — as lumbermill hand, stage hand in a burlesque theater, and reporter for the *Atlanta Journal* — he sold his first story in 1929. His novel *God's Little Acre* (1933) became a rip-roaring sucess when cleared of obscenity charges after 40 of America's best-known writers and critics testified that it was literature. The same year he received the Yale Review's $1,000 prize for "Country Full of Swedes." *Tobacco Road* (1932) was another successful novel about poor whites in Caldwell's native Georgia. He portrayed people the way they were, not as reformers would like them to be; but he never sneered at them. Many of his works are pervaded by a lyrical feeling for nature. Caldwell died in 1987.

A newly rising star in the science fiction field, baseball enthusiast **MICHAEL CASSUTT** lives in California, where he works for a television network. His stories are carefully crafted and often unusual. His first published story, "The Streak," was a detective tale about an attempt to murder a winning player and appeared in *Mike Shayne Mystery Magazine* in 1977. Soon Cassutt's work was being featured in *Omni* (with "The Holy Father," about a man who realizes his political ambitions are doomed when his son becomes able to work miracles) and *Universe 8,* and lately he has published longer stories in such magazines as *Isaac Asimov's Science Fiction Magazine.*

One of the few authors to be also a famous film actor, **IRVIN S. COBB** was born in Kentucky in 1876. Leaving high school after two years to make a living, he became reporter and managing editor (the country's youngest) on the *Paducah Daily News*. In 1901 he became the *New York Sun*'s columnist and later war correspondent, writing his first story in 1913. He and his wife left New York ("We tried it thirty-four years and we didn't like the place," he said) for California, where he wrote filmscripts and acted in such films as *Steamboat Round the Bend,* about a steamboat race on the Mississippi, with Will Rogers. His best-known books include *Old Judge Priest* (1915), filmed with Will Rogers; the humorous *Speaking of Operations* (1916); the title tale in *Faith, Hope, and Charity* (1934); and the grim story included here. He died in 1944.

ELLEN DOUGLAS was born Josephine Ayres in Natchez, Mississippi, in 1921 and attended schools at Hope, Arkansas, and Alexandria, Louisiana. She went to Randolph-Macon Women's College before transferring to the University of Mississippi, where she was graduated in 1942. She married Kenneth Haxton, Jr., of Greenville, Mississippi, with whom she had three sons. Her first novel, *A Family's Affairs* (1962), was awarded the Houghton Mifflin Award. Her story "On the Lake" was first published in *The New Yorker* and received recognition by being included in the O. Henry collection of best short stories of 1963. Later it became part of the novella *Hold On* and was included in Douglas's second book, *Black Cloud, White Cloud* (1964). Subsequent novels have included *Apostles of Light* (1973), *A Lifetime Burning* (1982), and most recently *Can't Quit You, Baby* (1988).

Born in Kentucky in 1795, **BENJAMIN DRAKE** had little formal education. A clerk and later partner in an uncle's general store in Cincinnati, Drake studied law in 1825 and 1826 and was a lawyer the rest of his life. He regularly contributed stories and articles to local papers, and writing soon became a second profession. He was editor of the *Cincinnati Chronicle* from 1826 to 1834 and author of *Cincinnati in 1826*, a non-fiction study valued by historians. Ill health compelled him to retire and he died in 1841. His best-known works include *Tales and Sketches from the Queen City* (1838) and the non-fiction *Life and Adventures of Black Hawk* (1838).

A little-known nineteenth-century author, **WILLIS GIBSON** published three short stories about steamboats on the Mississippi that revealed his knowledge of geography and steamboat operation. In addition, six of his articles dealing with engineering and the Mississippi were published between 1901 and 1903.

Noted for her historical stories and sketches of the Old South, **GRACE KING** was born in New Orleans in 1859 and educated there. When occupying Union forces moved into New Orleans in 1862, the King family moved north to New Iberia, Louisiana. They returned after the Civil War to find themselves penniless and forced to begin again. King's sketches in the *New Princeton Review* became the basis for her first novel, *Monsieur Motte* (1888). Her books, largely set against a background of Creole culture in New Orleans, include *Tales of a Time and Place* (1892), *Balcony Stories* (1892), and the non-fiction *DeSoto and His Men in the Land of Florida* (1898). She died in 1932; her stories have been collected in *Grace King of New Orleans* (Louisiana State University Press, 1986).

E.P. O'DONNELL was born in 1895 in New Orleans, Louisiana, of Irish-American parents. He began working while still in grammar school and held more than thirty jobs in his lifetime. He published short stories in *Harper's, Scribner's, Collier's,* and the *Yale Review.* His novels included *The Great Big Doorstep* (1941) and *Green Margins* (1946); for the latter he won a Houghton Mifflin Literary Fellowship. O'Donnell died in 1943.

WILLIAM JOSEPH SNELLING was born in Boston in 1804. His mother died in his youth; his father, an Army officer, sent him to West Point in 1818. Snelling hated the regimentation and left after two years to begin an adventurous and colorful life in the West. He lived among the Dakota people, became a fur trapper, married a French woman at Prairie du Chien who died their first winter there, and fought Indians in the Winnebago Revolt of 1827. After his father's death he returned to Boston to begin a literary career as reporter, reformer, and editor. He first gained attention for "Truth" (1831), a verse satirizing contemporary poets that scandalized Boston. As editor of the *New England Galaxy,* he crusaded against public evils usually successfully but at the cost of many friends and his health. Drink and personal misfortunes led to a four-month jail term. He became editor of the *Boston Herald* in 1847 but died the next year. Among his books are *Tales of the Northwest* (1830) and *The Rat-Trap* (1837).

E. EARL SPARLING was born in 1897. His short story collection *Under the Levee,* focusing on New Orleans and other Louisiana settings, appeared in 1925. Sparling also published more than a dozen articles in popular magazines of his day.